GW00858364

DANCING WI... ......

Portslade Penpushers

In memory of

Mike Whelan 1951 – 2013
Ray Haynes 1936 - 2012
Raymond Arthur Goldfinch 1924 - 2010
Kazimierz Sawicki 'Kaz' - 1914 - 2001

and all the patients at the Martlets
Hospice in Hove
past, present and to come.

This anthology is a tribute to the consultants and counsellors and charity shop workers, to the volunteers who donate their time and energy and the behind-the-scenes-team who make it all possible. It is a thank you to the nurses who know how to say the unsayable and give courage to patients and their families as they face the last journey.

It is always hard to part, but this is how it should end, with care and expert attention, with grace and dignity, and with love.

No one was paid to produce this anthology or claimed expenses. We pledge that every penny of profit from this book will go to the hospice. They need it. We need them.

A lot of people helped us make this book and promote it. We own them a big debt of gratitude and you will find their names in the acknowledgements section at the back. There is more information on our website http://strictlycomewriting.wordpress.com

DANCING WITH WORDS grew out of
creative writing classes at Portslade Adult
Learning, an education centre on the edge of
Brighton where the South Downs roll down to
meet the sea.

We thought that it would be interesting for
readers and useful for fellow writers to know the
source of each story. Some sprouted fully-
formed from a class exercise. Some were
inspired by a chance remark, some just
happened…. At the end of every chapter there is
a *Where Did that Come From?* section. We
hope it adds to your enjoyment and may even
help you on your own writing journey

Editor and Creative Writing Tutor: Bridget
Whelan

Authors: Charlie Bowker, Christine Maskell,
Hélène Meredith, Janis Thomson, João Sousa,
Julie Gibbons, Liz Carboni, Liz Tyrrell, Maggie
Wright, Martine Clark, Mary Goldfinch, Michael
Forrer, Pat Burt, Richard Shakesheff, Rosalind
Johnston, Sallie A Sawicka, Sally Wood

From the Vice Principal of PACA Adult Learning

We are excited to support this innovative and dynamic project. We are not only proud of this group's aim to raise money for such a good cause, but also of their artistic creativity and dynamism in getting this project off the ground.

We truly believe that Adult Learning can enrich lives by raising aspiration, releasing people to achieve their potential and enabling personal dreams and ambitions to be fulfilled.

This group is a real example of the transformational effect of Adult Learning.

Nick Fenn

Clayton Wood
for Mike Whelan
by Rosalind Johnston

Stillness;
The soft bleating of sheep
High on the hill,
Beneath the watching mills;
Jack and Jill.
Down in the hidden hollow, a sudden
Train on the shadowed track startles;
Shatters the quiet –
Its shocking clackety-clack fading back into
Silence.
A chill breeze stirs the saplings' leaves
To dance above the butterfly, buttercup meadow.
Yellow, yellow, yellow, the petals
Call down the anointing of night
Onto their close-lipped buds.
This is a wood in the making.
In this incised greensward
Your father, your lover,
Your son, your brother
Lies down; birthed, betrothed
To the new-dug earth of his narrow bed.
He is not alone; a corolla of graves
Flowers out from the meadow's heart.
A blossoming rod and staff of paths and names.
Written in the book of the coming wood
Is his name; indelibly inscribed
In the rings of future oak trees.
Just beyond the fences
The ancient woodland breathes and sways

In expectation of the rising body;
The longed-for chorus of skyward limbs.
Until then, be faithful.
Recite the litany of trees;
Let the sacred names speak him into the light –
Willow, rowan, hawthorn, ash and yew.

In Memory of Ray Haynes
by Martine Clarke

We were all there on your last night
When you could no longer fight.
We held your hand to let you know
We didn't want to let you go.
Now you are in a better place
But we will not forget your face.
You are with us in all we do
Thank you Ray for being you.

This Is Not Goodbye
for Raymond Arthur Goldfinch
by Mary Goldfinch

If I wanted to say goodbye to you,
How would I say that?
I must take care.
Some might be pleased if I said goodbye.
How careful should I be?
Some may smile. I will not say too much.
Some people might blush.
It is better to say too little than too much.
Some names bring happiness, others no
response.
I will say nothing.
I will not say goodbye to you, only others.
How could I dream of saying goodbye to you?
This is only to say to you I am not saying
goodbye.
It might have been goodbye.

Workman
for 'Kaz'
by Sallie A. Sawicka

Today he is a clumsy Russian bear
Morose, withdrawn, unlikeable, detached.
I pick my way around him with great care
His anger and my caution finely matched.
He was as active as a cub last week,

It seemed as if his summer had returned.
Today brings icy rain, the forest bleak,
A pile of rose bush cuttings lie unburned.
He sits cross-legged, cross patched with lowered head
And tries to mend the handle of a knife
Within the doorway of the garden shed
Surrounded by the clutter of his life.
He drops his tools, and curses in despair.
Today he is a clumsy Russian bear.

Where Did That Come From…?

Clayton Wood

Rosalind says: Clayton Wood is a Natural Burial Ground on the South Downs near Brighton, where individual graves bear saplings which will one day return the whole area to indigenous woodland. I was moved to write this poem one beautiful, June evening in 2009 when I visited the grave of a young family member who died unexpectedly. May he rest in peace!

Bridget says: Rosalind sent this poem to me after my husband died. She knew he had been buried in Clayton Wood and hoped it would be of some comfort. When I couldn't write myself and words seemed clumsy things, there was solace in reading something so beautiful.

In Memory of Ray Haynes
Martine says: the words were carefully chosen to hold Ray's memory dear. They came from the heart and were echoed by the many people who will always love my brother in law.

This Is Not Goodbye
Bridget says: one week the class read together Paul Hansford's poem *This Is Not A Poem* (read it and other poems by Paul at http://www.poemhunter.com) and for homework I asked students to write their own version – you can see other contributions on this theme elsewhere in the book. I remember that when Mary read it aloud in class no one spoke afterwards so powerful and genuine was the message.
I don't know if she was thinking of her late husband when she wrote it, perhaps she doesn't know herself, but we both agreed that it was the perfect choice when she was asked to write a dedication.

Workman
Sallie says: Kaz, my Polish husband, was between operations for cancer when I wrote this poem. There are very few bears in Poland but

Russian bears have a reputation for being clumsy, aggressive and unpredictable. This was how I saw Kaz as he tried to mend a knife handle with masking tape. He dropped the knife several times and then threw it down muttering under his breath, in Russian I expect. He always said Russians had the best swear words.

CONTENTS

There have been great societies that did not use the wheel, but there have been no societies that did not tell stories.
Ursula LeGuin

Bunny Hopping and Fox Trotting

You are always naked when you start writing; you are always as if you had never written anything before; you are always a beginner. Shakespeare wrote without knowing he would become Shakespeare. Erica Jong

Are Rabbits Ever Frigid?
João Sousa

Darwin had a Point
Janis Thomson

Penelope Barnum
Richard Shakesheff

The Snake in the Grass
Charlie Bowker

Are Rabbits Ever Frigid?
João Sousa

"No!" his voice was croaking, muffled by the right paw scratching his nose. His pointy head was always bent, but those little eyes vivid, moving, screening all directions that could hide surprise or danger.

Alfa Rabbit grouped the youngsters together and told them, with paw gestures across his face and pointing, that it was time they picked their own food. There is no school for rabbits other than the adventurous world where they had to survive. AR knew very well that the end result might well be a premature live cremation in some stew pot, or impalement on a stick and slow spiral dancing over a fire. The worse, he guessed, would be to play the role of victim on the teeth of several hunting dogs, torn into pieces under the complacent eyes of gentry and lady-ships riding well-polished, sweaty horses and dressed in strange garments.

AR was tired, very tired. Sleepless nights with all those litters bearing his coat pattern of curved spots on their fur. They were his, he had no doubt. Now and again Mrs Rabbit would enlarge her waist, slow her walking, bring less grass to the bolt hole. He had to work double to feed his offspring and their mother. They were a large family, but he could only count on himself. The older children left, looking for other pastures. He rarely received news of sightings. His relatives, dispersed to the neighbouring fields and farms, suffered the same strain: they couldn't help reproducing like rabbits.

Rabbits have no rights, he thought. We offer our children to the amusement and kitchens of humans. We adult rabbits too, sooner or later end our lives before our due time, murdered, slaughtered. We embody two great sadness of Mother Nature: we are proletarians – for what else do we have other than our children – and we are war casualties. Collateral damage!

When the night came, a cool wind filtered through their lodgings. Mrs Rabbit came closer to him to get herself warm. There, again, he thought. There. He looked around, the twilight of the full moon reaching their lodgings and counted the children: two were missing. Their siblings were quiet. Their mouse-like faces transpired terror. AR knew what they knew. He had not seen it happen. The method was not important; it was the permanent threat of humans and beasts that would cut their lives short, no warning. He felt cold. Too cold. He felt guilty, too. He could not protect his own.

He turned back to Mrs Rabbit, put a paw to her belly and the other on her back, and said, sounding Napoleonic and French, "Not tonight, darling."

Darwin had a Point

Janis Thomson

He was different. An enigma. When people asked where he came from he would say Central America and, if pushed, Ecuador. No more than that. Roberto was the sole beneficiary of a successful family business and he lived alone in the family house in Hampstead. Swimming and diving were his first loves, with an obsession for shoes coming a very close second.

He had recently introduced fish to his indoor salt water pool and as he dived gracefully, nose forward, he would target an unsuspecting victim and haul it proudly to the surface. The rest of his time was spent bidding on eBay for unusual footwear, vintage or contemporary. His most treasured possession was a pair of genuine Elvis blue suede creepers which he had won in a fierce online bidding war against an enthusiastic American.

Roberto's social life was not successful. At social events his beady eye would turn downwards and he would scan the room for a likely candidate with unusual foot attire, never lifting his gaze. At times he had been rounded on by outraged groups of women accusing him of leg-ogling. All this was most unfortunate, particularly because, when excited, he would stamp up and down, rather like a seagull.

Roberto was drawn to the sea and frequently visited Brighton where anything went. He felt at one with the endless expanse of water and the presence of seagulls all around him. He always booked a deluxe suite at The Grand, overlooking the sea. On this occasion the weather was perfect and the sea calm. There were many people and activities along the promenade, but Roberto stamped along in his blue suede shoes unaware, eyes steadfastly fixed at ankle position.

And then suddenly he was transfixed by a woman's legs approaching in vintage Jimmy Choo's. Blue! Simultaneously their eyes slid upwards and the attraction and recognition was instantaneous. Immediate! Thrilling! Roberto's feet danced uncontrollably and the woman smiled. No words were needed. At last he had found his soul mate. Silently they padded back to the hotel, unaware of amused onlookers. They hopped into Roberto's sports car and headed back to London. To his pool. They dis-robed, both proudly displaying blue, slightly webbed, feet. The mating dance of the blue-footed boobies began…

Penelope Barnum
Richard Shakesheff

Penelope Barnum grew up in Edinburgh, the only child of parents who she described as distant and unaffectionate. Nel, as she liked to be called, went on to study a History of Art at

Brighton University, just about as far from Scotland as she could get. Whilst she didn't excel on the course, she loved the student life, and blossomed into a very handsome young woman. With long blond hair, deep blue eyes, high cheek bones and an athletic body, she turned men's heads wherever she went.

Along with her good looks, she portrayed herself as vulnerable yet funny, a mixture her fellow male students and lecturers found intoxicating. Females always saw through her charms, but this didn't stop her having a close circle of friends, all keen to have some of her magic rub off on them.

During her time at Uni, Nel had a string of boyfriends, most relationships lasting just a week a two, when she became bored. She would break men's hearts like egg shells, leaving hollow husks in her wake. One such suitor, a promising physics student was so shattered by the break up, he immediately packed his bags, left University and returned to Swindon, where he took a job in a fish and chip shop. One of her lecturers had become so beguiled that it poisoned his life. He left his wife and children for Nel in the first week of their fling. By the second week it was over and he was alone, ashamed and living in a squalid studio flat at Preston Circus.

After leaving Uni, Nel got a job in Brighton, selling advertising space in a property paper. It was on a girls' night out with two of her Uni friends, Lizzie and Kerry, when Nel fell in love.

Marcus Bailey was in town on a stag night, having travelled down from London. He was ten years older than Nel, tall, handsome, and above all else, rich. She could tell that right away by his clothes, and the way he spent stupid amounts of money on champagne. She was impressed.

Within three months they were engaged. She persuaded him to sell his swanky bachelor pad in London, complete with home cinema and shared pool, so they could have their own place in Brighton. A grand house, by Hove Park, she furnished and decorated to her own taste.

Within a month of their marriage, the now Mrs. Nel Barnum - Bailey, fell pregnant with twins. As some women do in pregnancy, Nel began to eat. She developed a love of iced buns and tea at first, and the weight began to pile on. When Marcus tired of the daily commute, he found himself staying up in Town more and more, leaving his precious Nelly at home. The long sleepless nights and loneliness saw her baby blue eyes turn red and swollen.

After the twins were born, things came to a head. Marcus had an offer of promotion, and a move to the Hong Kong office. Nelly put her foot down and refused to go, Marcus equally stubbornly refused to budge, so they agreed he would come home every six weeks. He rarely did.

Now nearly thrice the weight she had been before marriage, her legs puffed up, the bronze skin now had a greyness about it. She no longer shaved her legs, and tufts of thick black hair sprouted. Her long blonde hair was now cropped and brown.

A chance exchange of emails saw Nelly inviting her old friends Lizzie and Kerry round for tea. With the table set, a plate of iced buns at the centre, she opened the front door to the beaming smiles of her friends. The smiles became fixed and false in a state of horror when they saw what their friend now looked like.

Nelly ushered the girls into the dining room, and poured the tea. Sitting back in her chair, Nelly dunked her trunk in the sweet, hot drink and then squirted the contents into her mouth.

Kerry and Lizzie sat ashen faced, speechless, neither one wanting to mention the elephant in the room.

The Snake in the Grass
Charlie Bowker

He was a slippery, tricky man. Yes, he was dressed in an elegant, well-tailored suit, complete with waistcoat and a red neckerchief. He wore pince-nez spectacles at the end of his nose which gave him an intelligent, focussed look, but the thin, wiry man behind the clothes added up to something very different.

You would meet him on the race course. Whether you wanted to or not, he would ease up to you, and greet you like a long lost friend with an oily sticky shake of the hand, whether you wanted to or not. Your partner would slip away as soon as she decently could, leaving you to front the rash of platitudes and unfunny remarks trickling from his mouth. Often there would be the remains of spittle at the end of his mouth after a run of unfunny jokes had left him spluttering at his own cleverness.

Inevitably, he would insist on a horse he could get at ten-to-one, but the bookies were all offering at fives. This was a sure-fire winner he would hiss, brooking no contradiction. Several people had been caught out by his insistence and lost considerable sums of money, but he would wriggle his way out of their confrontations, insist you had backed the wrong horse, whilst crowing about the five that he had backed but hadn't mentioned to you, making him thousands.

He was the classic unwanted guest, always wriggling his way into a gathering or party without an invitation. Then, impervious to the general sense of unease, he would carry on as though he was the life and soul of the party, drink a disproportionate share of the drink, and leave after everyone else.

Charge of the Heavy Brigade
Christine Maskell

He stood in the middle of his front garden,
harrumphing indignantly at the group of boys
who were dancing and jeering at him from the
pavement. He peered short-sightedly through
ridiculously small, round glasses, perched
precariously at the end of his very large nose, at
the football he was holding in his large hand and
again at the boys. The boldest ventured to the
front gate to ask for the ball back.

He looked around, slowly, but could see no
damage. Even so, the boys represented a
danger of sorts; he didn't like them so close to
his territory. With surprising speed for a man of
his large girth, he hunched his shoulders and
launched himself towards the nearest boy, who
very quickly decided that retreat was the better
part of valour and ran up the road.

Angered and frustrated now, he turned his
attention to the other boys, and charged towards
them, watching them flee with some satisfaction.
He ambled back to his garden, and didn't notice
that the ball was no longer there. Were these the
same boys that had pointed and laughed at him
yesterday he wondered, or were they different
ones? It didn't matter; everyone was cautious
about setting foot in his garden. Ever since the
day he had managed to catch up with one of the
boys and sent him flying with a head butt. It
caused a stir in the street all right, but what the

hell! He didn't care what people said about him! With that, he headed toward his front door, it was food time again and a lovely fresh salad waiting to be eaten.

Dog's life
João Sousa

Hi. I don't bark, no. I roar. Loud. Loud, not clear, but damn loud! I roar.

My size is above average! A lion-size canine with the heart of a king. King of the urban jungle. I might be only three years old, but I know my ways. Life has hardened me. I earned my rank and stripes in the neighbourhood of suburban gardens, flowerbeds, edges, shrubs, low rise fences. Canines are supposed to be tough, rough, feared. No, nowadays we are 'pets', can you believe it? Domestic pets!

Wrong! Cats are pets. They have collars, but no leads. They stay home and always come back home. They are cats, what would you expect? Dwarf size they are. Silly. Never have a bath, can you believe it? Many have been spayed. No more night serenades by January's moonlight. A timid tail that can stand on the vertical, but when I come into sight, no tail to be seen and soon no feline to be seen, either. Hum.

How I like to see them run. Run forward. Run upwards for refuge, up the trees, up the walls, up the roofs. Pets? Pests, I call them.

But other fellow dogs, too, are a pitiful sight. Haircuts, hair brushed, winter waistcoats! And neutered too! How dare they! A dog is a dog, is a dog, is a full dog. No pieces missing! Some, even the tail, has been deleted! How can a true dog express himself without a tail? Do Italians talk without their hands? Nonsense. Now listen here, I am telling you, I am complete. Tail. Male bits. No haircut. No nonsense.

My so-called owner – so he thinks, rather call him my sponsor - takes me for walks twice a day, and, very obedient, collects my poo. It is his job. Thinks he's in charge. Makes me run in the park to catch balls. Thinks the exercise keeps me fit. It's me that makes him walk, walk, walk, to lose weight. Reverse psychology. Serves him right. I am fit. I-am-a-dog! But I oblige. It is a part of our social contract.

Makes me feel stupid, it does. As revenge, I poo in places of difficult access. I am supposed to do my…release in full view of whoever is around. He doesn't. He's got his dignity. I've got mine too. So I go into the bushes where there is enough space for me to enter, but not enough for him. He gets a hard time, he does. Scratched by branches and thorns, just to collect my…rejections. Good boy. Civilized he is. So he thinks. Then I play him, my brow up, the tail giggling in the air, a bit of barking, *sotto voce* to reward him. The kind, friendly face he makes, carrying my poo. Dear, dear.

He bubbles a bit of friendly nonsense about me to other dogs' enslavers who trail their miserable pets, necks restrained by collars and leads. My approach is surreptitious. I come near, closer and then have a go at those furry aberrations, submissive traitors of the canine tribe. Terror. I do strike terror! See terror in their eyes, their hair standing as if stricken by lightning. Their legs bending backwards, their eyes imploring pity, their wills gone into thin air.

Then, I change my act. Sniff around friendly. Leak them, even. But they know. Oh, they do know. Supremacy counts. Little bastards. Sons of bitches, like me. But that's all we've got in common. For I am my father's son, whichever dog he was.

The Mouse's Tail
Hélène Meredith

His wife was always telling him not to be so timid.

Stan hated the limelight and found it difficult to make decisions, quite content spending time sitting by the fire, reading books. Unfortunately his life was turned into misery by Irene's constant bickering. She spent most days criticising him, urging him to be more useful around the house.

He longed for some peace and quiet. There was the shed at the bottom of the garden, but it was not far enough from the house. He could still hear her voice calling him and, if he did not reply, she would run down the path to see what he was up to. Sitting in the old armchair he had rescued from one of his wife's drastic clear-outs, he had that weird fantasy that if he could somehow shrink, he would be able to hide from her. With that recurring thought in mind, he decided to go to bed early to escape his wife's nagging.

The next morning, Stan woke up feeling all out of sorts and wondering where he was. He was lost in a sea of sheets and could not find his way out. His sense of smell seemed to have heightened overnight and he had a strong desire to eat cheese for breakfast. He looked at the tall mirror at the bottom of the bed and caught a glimpse of some rodent-like creature. Surely it could not be... Assuming it was him he was looking at, he had shrunk into a little dormouse with rounded ears, velvety fur and a bushy tail. Large dark eyes stared at him in the mirror. Stan hid under the sheet then came out again, hoping it was just a dream, but the mouse was still there. He tried to remember if anything strange had happened the night before but all he could think off was that he had wished he was small enough to hide from his wife.

Stan felt quite vulnerable but managed to run down the length of the bed awkwardly and reach the carpet. Going down the stairs was another matter. The quickest way would be to slide down the banister but it might be quite traumatic for a little mouse. Plucking his courage, he just gripped his paws onto the wood and hoped for the best. Still in a daze after his performance all he could see was huge brown slippers coming towards him.

'Stan, where are you?' shouted Irene.

Should he let on what had happened to him or keep quiet? He decided he had to tell his wife before she trampled him by accident or worried herself to death about his sudden disappearance.

'Stan, where are you?' she called again.

A squeaky voice came from underneath the kitchen table. 'I am here dear.'

'Where?'

'Under the table,' said Stan.

Irene bent down. When she saw the mouse, she jumped on the kitchen chair.

'Irene, it's me,' said the squeaky voice.

She looked again in disbelief. 'Stan, is that really you?'

'Yes, dear, I don't know what happened to me but I woke up as a mouse. You'd better put the cat outside before he makes a meal of me.'

Irene was more worried about the neighbours. Who'd ever hear of a talking mouse apart from Mickey or the Tom and Jerry's cartoons on the TV? Should she call the doctor?

He probably would say that she was the one in need of medical attention.

'Irene,' said the squeaky voice, 'if it's not too much trouble, could you give me a bit of cheese, my stomach is rumbling. I haven't had any breakfast.'

Irene summoned up her courage and gave the mouse a crumb of cheese. Then she got a shoe box out of the cupboard. 'Here, you better climb in there for the time being, you'll be safer.'

Over the coming weeks, the couple had to curtail drastically their social life, no more dinner parties or playing bridge with the neighbours. Irene gave the cat to some friends as Stan was not safe with it around the house. They slowly got used to a new way of living. Irene told the neighbours her husband was away visiting his sister in Cardiff. For Stan, being a mouse had its advantages. He could disappear when he wanted to, usually having a snooze in the fir trees in the garden. He came back inside the house when he felt like it. When they went out shopping, Stan could easily fit into Irene's large coat pocket and she was careful not to squash him. Irene, always the practical one, had even hinted that if they wanted to go on holiday, they would only need to pay for one ticket.

That state of affairs lasted for three weeks until one morning, Stan somehow got back to his former self after drinking half a cup of herbal tea Irene had left in the kitchen. He was relieved to be human again if only to be able to play bridge with the neighbours or have a decent meal. He swore he'd never wish for his body to shrink again. Irene became more patient with him and did not complain so much. Stan had finally learned to stand his ground when Irene was overstepping the mark. To get away from her he started going once a week to an evening class on Sussex wildlife.

Sugar and Spice and All Things Nice
Pat Burt

Her mind was in a whirl - her hero, her Prince Charming, had asked her to stay behind after the meeting. The looks from the leggy, blonde beauties who bedecked the offices were a joy. What had caught his eye? Certainly not her slightly dumpy figure, perhaps the glossy black hair, brilliant smile or the overwhelming wish to please that her personality exuded. She would do anything for him and anything was what she did.

There were secret meetings, accidental brushing of hands and moments of intimacy in the innermost sanctum. People began to notice. She glowed and made excuses to visit his office where she would linger just that bit too long.

Finally, the confrontation came from her closest friend. The beans were spilled and secretly recorded. Keep everything was the message.

"Even the blue dress?"

"Especially the blue dress, and the cigar." As always, wanting to please, she did as she was told. Then the crash came.

"Do not sign that affidavit."

The denials, the lies. Her bewilderment. Why had he done this? He loved her.

The world crumbled around her. Not understanding what had happened or why, she was like a loyal and loving puppy left by the roadside.

The Neighbours
Liz Tyrrell

He was usually to be seen at dusk trotting towards one or another of his relations. In our neighbourhood of tightly packed houses his family enjoyed even greater proximity. They all seemed to live in their own little ghetto, the residences standing back to back or being linked by gloomy alleys or muddy paths. Toilets and wash houses punctuated the grid. Bushes met overhead to form tunnels. It had been the same, apparently, since anyone remembered, passed from one generation to the next.

The Old Man was definitely the head of the clan and obviously very ancient. We were fascinated by his hair. We knew it must be dyed and chuckled from an upstairs window at the central white stripe dividing that glossy black head.

Daytime was a mystery but those households certainly came to life at night. Neighbours had complained about noise, music and laughter into the small hours. They toned it down after that but, if you couldn't sleep, you would look out and always see their houses ablaze with light. They'd been observed in the woods at midnight flashing torches and foraging for food. Very fond of DIY too, which, of course, they did after dark. Curtains closed during the day.

They didn't mix with the rest of the community, "kept themselves to themselves" as neighbours are fond of saying. Aware of cooking smells and sounds of revelry one night I crept downstairs and along one of the alleys where I pressed my face to the hedge. Through a gap I watched in astonishment as all sorts of food was wolfed down from steaming pots, meat, vegetables, what looked like *wild flowers* and over everything the tangy smell of cooking rabbit.

At twilight on the day that we all received the fateful letter we watched him lumbering from dwelling to dwelling, agitated, breathless, flapping the paper.

We'd all been shocked. I barely understood my parents' mutterings of 'Compulsory purchase...demolition...motorway....', but there was no mistaking the sounds of panic and grief as the Brocks wailed into the night sky.

The Quiet Teacher
Michael Forrer

Geoffrey looked across the staff room, his beady eyes fixed on the Deputy Head's salad lunch. He had taught at the school for many years – his second job since arriving from South America with some of the best references and qualifications you could hope to see. The Deputy Head glanced up and remembered when she first shook his hand - so surprisingly cold.

Geoffrey's hair hung forward in a rough-cut fringe keeping it well clear of those eyes. He wore a ragged thick woolly jumper – a grey brown mixture - much the same colour as his hair. And in summer if you caught a glimpse of his hairy arms you saw how wiry thin he was. Bones and tendons covered by skin –virtually no fat and only a hint of muscle.

Geoffrey looked hungry but ate little. He rose from his chair so cautiously that he remained unnoticed by the other teachers. He crept across the room to extract a small white plastic box from his locker. When, eventually, he sat he carefully opened the lid and slowly devoured two leaves of lettuce and an insignificant piece of chicken.

Lunch over, Geoffrey made his way back to the jungle of tough teenagers. In class those beady eyes kept constant watch. He turned his back and began to write on the whiteboard giving thought to every letter. His thumb and two fingers grasped the marker pen tightly, as if to squeeze out the last remaining drop of blue ink. Few dared ask how he had lost his two littlest fingers and those who did just received a moment's silent blank stare. Even with his back to the class Geoffrey could hear the gentlest opening of a desk or the most secret whisper. Then he would demonstrate his amazing ability to twist his neck a full three quarter circle and pick out a pupil in the furthest corner.

He was more at home in this classroom than in the staff room with the other teachers. He was master of his subject and of his class. And there, although he said little and never raised his voice, he earned respect.

Life On The Edge
Liz Carboni

He straightened his collar in that jerky way he always did, pushed back his hair over his left ear, and felt the slight movement of his medallion against his chest. He was looking good.

His life on the street was on the edge, he carried himself with the confidence of youth and with the assurance that his sartorial elegance was unsurpassed. His carefully selected gang - their tag was the Lancers - arrived in dribs and drabs, some looking positively unwashed but ready to hang on his every word. He was a born leader, but cocky with it and a few of the older guys would slap him down occasionally.

Today they followed their usual routine, checked out some cars, tried a few back doors and then regrouped by the statue. He sat on the top of the artistic lump, with his long legs, encased in stripped skinny jeans, hanging over the side. Boring, boring, boring!

Missing. He was missing. He told no one of his intentions, took no one with him and left fear and consternation in the space that was his. The gang - even the oldies - called by his house several times a day, just to see if he was back. Words like *bad company, drugs* and hushed references to the Mafia were heard.

Four nights later he was found, his beautiful hair was a matted mess of white powder, his nails chewed down to the quick and traces of blood caked the soft down on his chest. The old ones spotted him first and sent the Lancers in to view him and learn from his pitiful state. They knew what had happened, one or two of them had been to that place too. A mistake that big was going to take him down a peg or two.

Prozac was prescribed to calm him and erase the dreadful memories of his ordeal. The woman who loved him washed him, tended his bitten body and rejoiced in his return. It was some weeks before he ventured out.

Where Did That Come From…?

Bridget says: most of the stories in this section came from a homework assignment. Each student was asked to research an animal and base a human character on what they discovered.

For example, Geoffrey in The Quiet Teacher is really a sloth under that thick woolly jumper. Michael's research notes include the fact that their stomachs act so slowly it can take a month to fully digest a meal and they have the lowest metabolic rate of any mammal of their size. Geoffrey's cold hands come from a normal body temperature of between 86 to 93 degrees. Like sloths he has untidy brown grey hair, a woolly coat and small eyes. Like sloths, he has very little muscle mass - they are known to continue gripping onto a tree branch after death.

Are Rabbits Ever Frigid?

Bridget says: post-it notes are very useful for writing exercises and on this occasion class members had to jot down a story title they had just invented and stick it on the whiteboard, safe in the knowledge that someone else would have to write it up. João wrote the story and Pat Burt came up with the title.

Darwin Had a Point

Jan says: The blue footed booby story is from an exercise on metamorphosis. I'd been lucky enough to go to the Galapagos Islands and fell in love with these funny little birds.

Penelope Barnum

Richard says: Penelope Barnum was inspired by *Lady Into Fox* – extracts were read in class. Mine is more comedy than drama, and got a laugh on the day.

Bridget says: David Garnett, a Brighton born member of the Bloomsbury Set, wrote *Lady into Fox* in 1922. It is an extraordinary allegory that the reader is left to interpret.

Dog's life

João says: one does not need to believe in rebirth or reincarnation to be sensitive to the plight of animals and find the similarities with our own behaviour and mind frames.

Life On The Edge

Liz says: my spotty, stripy ginger and black Bengal cat was locked in a painter's van over a long weekend. It calmed him.

Dancing in the Dark

We make up horrors to help us cope with the real ones. Stephen King

A Sussex Murder Story
by the A Team

Street Singer
Sallie A. Sawicka

The Old Tenement Block
Richard Shakesheff

Safety First
Pat Burt

The Rival
Liz Tyrrell

Retribution
Christine Maskell

A Sussex Murder Story
by The A Team

aka Charlie Bowker, Christine Maskell, Helene Meredith, Martine Clark, Mary Goldfinch, Pat Burt and Bridget Whelan

"I'm tired of all this skulking around, Maggie, not knowing when I'm going to see you, not being able to go out in case we're seen together," my lover said, pacing up and down the bedroom in front of me, naked, a glass of red wine in one hand.

"I want a girlfriend I can show off to my friends, I want marriage, kids, the whole thing. If you can't or won't consider that, then it's over between us"

Kids! That was the last thing on my mind. Been there, got the T-shirt.

I left as soon as we were both dressed and stood waiting impatiently outside the block of flats for the taxi to come, remembering Geoff's words. My carefully arranged romantic evening had turned into a nightmare. First, Geoff stating he wanted to "settle down" and then his ultimatum. He's hinted at this before, but I've always been able to persuade him that it wasn't a good idea; that it was all too complicated and I would probably have to walk away from my marriage with absolutely nothing.

Although I didn't want our affair to end, I also liked the large house in the country, the foreign holidays and the social life a successful musician was able to offer. If Simon hadn't been such a dullard, I never would have been attracted to Geoff, but every marriage has its downside and I had thought my solution was perfect. We had been in bed, me hoping I would be able to make Geoff forget all about planning our future together, when my phone rang. I told Geoff I'd ignore it, but he insisted I answer it. One look at the screen told me it was my son. I was shocked: he'd never rung before and my hand shook as I held the phone to my ear. He said he was feeling ill, that his heart was racing. He'd been with some friends and had a few drinks so maybe one of them had been spiked. That made me really anxious and I told Geoff that I had to leave. He accused me of avoiding the issue yet again. I tried to explain to him how neat our current arrangements were, but he was having none of it and we ended up arguing.

We've never rowed, not once, but tonight, probably because I was concerned about my son, I accused him of being totally unreasonable, especially as he had made no mention of me bringing my 17 year old with me if I were to leave Simon. In the end, I told him he could stick his offer of a lift home and ordered a taxi. And that's why I'm stuck here, waiting for the blasted thing to come.

oOo

Another lousy meal - too busy dolling herself up to go out with one of her silly girlfriends, thought Simon as he studied himself in the mirror. That woman could burn air. I've tried, oh how I've tried. Even paid for that posh cookery course.

Simon smirked at his reflection. Thank goodness for Irena. Now there's a woman who knows the way to a man's heart. Not only that, she loves my music, the way I look, dress - she loves me. He smoothed back his thick, grey hair. Not bad for forty-eight, he thought. Irena has given me a new lease of life and what do I get from Maggie? Nothing!

Oh yes, she'll come to my gigs when she thinks there will be someone famous there. Then she can boast to her friends about how she chatted with Mick Jagger. Chatted with Mick Jagger - I don't think so. She passed him once in the corridor and said, "hallo".

He laughed without humour at the memory, but his smile brightened when he remembered the first time he decided to eat at the Goat and Compass. He couldn't recall what had brought him there. Fate, probably. How to fall in love with a Shepherd's Pie and then the cook, he thought. When he poked his head into the kitchen to compliment her, she had recognised him. Even had some of his CDs.

From then on he couldn't care less how many times Maggie went out. It was his son he worried about. If he left, it would mean leaving the boy on his own with his mother. Still, he thought, it was only another couple of years before he'll be independent and off and so will I. The idea gave him a warm glow. My marriage is staler than last week's bread and has been for years. He reflected on how it had started, not with starry eyes and high hopes, but with a drunken one night stand, a positive pregnancy test and a grubby blackmailing father who had enough contacts in the music industry to ruin him. Enough to put you off sex for life, he decided, which it had...almost.

So I'm off to rehearse with the lads - I don't think. He winked at his reflection in the mirror. If that keeps Maggie happy, so be it. He whistled as he went out. The boy was at a pal's house and he had an evening at The Goat and Compass ahead of him. Things weren't perfect but right now, this evening, they were ok. More than a bit ok.

oOo

I am really tired of living on my own in this rather sad basement flat on the sea front, just down from the posh bit on Marine Drive...I watch everyone coming down to Brighton with joy in their hearts and a party on their minds and all I've really got to show for my time here is this snatched affair with Maggie.

Yes, it's great when we meet up. Yes, she's a great lady, we have so much in common and enjoy laughing together and sleeping together...but then there are the spaces in between when she is back with her family. She's safe and secure, but what about me? I'm on my own. I don't have a special person for weekends and I worry whether the famous Simon won't find out and insist that she comes back to him. Then I get dropped and I sit here like a mug asking what was all that about?

I don't fancy starting again. The years are slipping by. I watch my friends engaged with their families, with a life committed and planned out, but me and Maggie haven't even reached second base; the family. Imagine if she got pregnant. The row that would cause! Would she leave him for me?

She says she's bored with the famous Simon and their sex life is over. But I don't want another four or five years of 'Will she? Won't she?' only to find that I'm out in the cold and over the hill at 50. I can't go on like this: either she leaves him or it is over for us. It's tearing me apart weekly.

oOo

The taxi driver pulled into the kerb and eyed the attractive middle aged woman waiting for him. This has to be my last fare of the night, he thought. I've been driving around Brighton all day, doing more than I legally should. He grimaced as he calculated how much he had made that week and how much more he needed to make. "That evil bitch." He got some pleasure from saying the words out loud and he thought of his ex-wife as he turned out the hire light. I never could earn enough to satisfy her when we were married and I still can't. She's destroying me. The threat is always the children. Give me more money or you don't see them.

He painted a smile on his face as he opened the door for his passenger and studied her more closely. Expensive hair. Good clothes. I've landed a nice one for my last fare, he decided.

"Yes, Missus I do happen to know the way to Ditchling. Miracle, isn't it?"

oOo

I'm no good at arguments and I was already regretting the little scene with Geoff when the taxi pulled up. As soon as I had made sure the driver knew where to go (so many of them have no idea anywhere outside town) I phoned Geoff. The phone seemed to ring for ages before he picked up and when I said I was sorry, he sounded quite cold.

No "love you Maggie". No "miss you Maggie". So, maybe this is the end after all.

oOo

She rung! She rung! I wasn't going to answer it. I was scared Maggie was going to tell me she was never going to see me again and I couldn't bear that. But she was all right and I could tell she was sorry.

I was a bit cagey, a bit cool. She has to know that I meant what I said. Perhaps she's thinking about our future together right now, perhaps even as she speeds along those winding Sussex roads she's thinking about how she will break the news.

But what about her son? I don't want him living with us, blaming me for breaking up the marriage. His father is not going to cope well with this to put it mildly. If we stayed in Brighton we could have no end of aggravation from the pair of them. No, I don't fancy being the wicked stepfather for years. We could leave Brighton and the wonderful Simon with his bleeding endless guitar strumming and start again in the West Country. There's a good English department at the University of Exeter and I'm sure I could get a job there as a lecturer after my experience at Sussex. I'm really fond of Dartmouth and Torquay and I've got family connections going back to my childhood there.

We could invite the boy down at the weekends, sometimes. The rest of the time he could live with Simon. That way he wouldn't feel he had lost everything and Maggie could go up to see her boy whenever she wanted.

To be honest I don't really like what I hear about him and I'm not much good with teenagers. I prefer to teach committed, well sorted out young adults getting into their twenties; not mop up all this acting out behaviour you see kicking off all over the streets and pubs.

Maggie rang me. It's going to be all right.

oOo

The taxi driver chewed his lip as he relived the day his wife went off with the local landlord who owned half the village where they had lived. He's got so much money, he thought, but it's never going to be enough for her. He's got my kids and my wife and she's still screwing me for maintenance. I did nothing wrong except work long hours to give her a good life. When we first got together I was an artist and sometimes I'd earn a lot for one commission and sometimes I'd earn nothing, she knew that, said she could accept it because she loved me. That didn't last long.

He pulled away from the kerb and drove towards the Old Steine. A group of drunk teenagers stumbled across the road, shrieking with laughter. He swore at them under his breath as he turned toward Lewes Road. His mind was still churning over the past as he drove out of Brighton. I took on taxi driving so she had a good life style, so she could up keep up with her phoney friends. What a joke! First opportunity she got, she went off with a man with more.

He tilted the mirror so he could get a better look at the woman in the back of his cab. In the glow from street lights he could see she was crying. Her face was blotchy and her mascara had run. Oh God, he thought, I don't need this. My last fare of this long, long, night.

I'm not going to talk to her, he decided. I'm not interested in her problems. She's going on and on, nagging at me to drive faster. She's got to get home because her boy's sick and her husband will go crazy if he finds out where she's been. The bitch.

oOo

I was so caught up in the hurt and misery of the whole thing that before I knew what had happened, I leaned forward and unburdened myself to the taxi driver. He hadn't said a word throughout my sorry tale and it was difficult to see his reaction because by now we were out of the town and onto the winding country road that led towards our village. I leaned forward and asked him how much the fare would cost, I had no idea and wasn't sure whether I had enough money on me. If my husband were home he would wonder as he thought I was only in the next village.

"So your husband has no idea about the affair?" he asked.

"No, of course not."

"What would happen if he did?" he asked.

"God, he'd probably throw me out," I said as the taxi pulled into a lay-by. "Why are you stopping?"

"I think you and I have a little negotiating to do," said the taxi driver. "How about doubling the fare in return for my silence? Of course, if you haven't got that kind of money on you, we could always reach some other sort of agreement. It's nice and private here and I'm willing to waive the fare in return for a quickie."

I was stunned. It wasn't as though I was attracted to him. Well, to be honest, until that moment I hadn't really looked at him, I'd just talked to the back of his head. I rifled through my bag for my purse and flung what notes I had towards him.

"Thanks, but no thanks," I said scrambling out of the cab. "I'll walk from here"

oOo

Where is Mum?

I don't know what's wrong with me, but my heart's pounding and I feel quite faint. Maybe it's something to do with that drink I had at that party earlier. I hope it wasn't spiked. Maybe I should drink some more water.

I rang Mum. She said not to bother her when she's with her friend, but I felt really weird, as if I was going to pass out. She sounded funny on the phone too, a bit flustered.

Could you please come back to the house? I said. She said she would, but it might take her awhile as she didn't take the car.

I think I need to lie down. Where is Mum?

oOo

Without a backward look at the taxi or the creep in the driving seat, I set off down the dark country road. The taxi's lights continued to illuminate the road ahead for a few minutes until I reached a bend, when they were obliterated. It took me a few moments to adjust to the darkness and the silence, which wasn't really silent at all. There were all sorts of rustling noises, which made me a feel a little nervous. I looked over my shoulder. My shoes were uncomfortable, and I decided to take them off and walk barefoot. I bent to remove them and that's when I heard a sound. Running feet and something else, something much closer: a voice, a whispering, simpering voice from somewhere to my right. Saying things, I'm not sure what exactly, but the sound of that voice was enough to make me run.

Until the world went black.

oOo

I've had enough, the taxi driver thought, slamming his fist into the windscreen. I could hurt this woman. Inflict pain she would remember for the rest of her life. I look at her and I see my wife.

She jumped out of my cab like I was something dirty and then starting throwing money around like my bitch of a wife. She is my wife. How dare she walk away? In the dark spaces of the taxi driver's mind, he knew she wasn't his wife, but he no longer cared: she was still a whore, a home breaker, a life-shatterer.

He turned off the lights and got out of his cab. He heard her footsteps at first, but then nothing, just rustling in the hedges. He began to run, determined to get her, to hurt her.

oOo

The man at the edge of the road had run out of petrol and was walking home to his wife and children. He had lost his mobile and was unable to ring the AA. He was annoyed with himself for not checking the car before he left Gatwick. After he had been walking for about ten minutes he saw a woman walking ahead and guessed she was about 40. He quickened his pace but kept to the shadows. Perhaps we can talk as we walk along, he thought. Perhaps she'll be a new friend.

"I left my car about half a mile down the road." She kept on walking in silence, but her pace quickened. The man tried again to get a response. After all, he thought, she is quite well dressed even though her hair wasn't very tidy. He could see her in the moonlight.

"I have got to walk about another two miles to my house. How far have you got to go?" he asked. Silence. He was growing rather cross with this stranger. So, not a friend just when he would have liked one. Just when he would have liked to feel the soft skin of her hand and walk with her into the darkness. She was running now. It was easy to keep up. It wasn't fair: he only wanted to be friends.

Suddenly, he saw a thick branch on the grass verge of the road. It must have blown down in last week's summer storm, he thought. He picked it up and felt the weight in his hand. He looked at the branch and the woman in front of him. Without thinking, he swung his arm and hit her on the head.

She fell onto the side of the road and lay motionless as blood poured across the tarmac. I don't understand why that happened. He frowned at the woman as if it was her fault. All she had to do was say hello and take his hand. At that moment he heard footsteps. He made his way quietly into the trees. The undergrowth was thick and he knew how to stand still for a long time. He liked standing still.

oOo

The taxi driver was running, determined to get to the woman. Suddenly he saw her slumped on the other side of the road. Good, he thought. Now lady, you are going to pay. He assumed she had stumbled but when he reached her all he could see was her staring eyes. There was a full moon and she was staring through him, blood covering her battered head. Someone else had got to her in those few moments, he realised.

oOo

The man in the shadows had good hearing and was the first to hear the car approaching. It seemed to him to be coming quite fast. Then it slowed down. The policemen got out and looked at the woman stretched out at the side of the road. The man held his breath as one of the policeman felt her pulse

oOo

When the police handcuffed the stunned taxi-driver, he kept repeating I didn't do it, over and over.

The policeman didn't reply and the taxi driver turned his face to the black night. He thought he saw a movement in the trees, but didn't say anything. There didn't seem much point.

Street Singer
Sallie A. Sawicka

My devils come to me and say it's day.
I know that it is night, but up I stand.
When my tormentors call I must obey,
The pills for my defence slip through my hand.
I look and now I hold a can of beer,
I fumble through my bedding and my rags;
My voices made my tablets disappear
To one of half-a-dozen plastic bags.
The dosser sleeping by my side tonight
Wakes up and curses that I sing and shout.
My visitors are laughing at my plight.
My human friend would like to kick me out.

I sing that Freedom is too big, too wide,
My devils slept when I was locked inside.

The Old Tenement Block
Richard Shakesheff

I didn't care who had lived in the building before. It was in a desirable neighbourhood on the Upper East Side, and my apartment had fantastic views of the park.

Being a lawyer I dealt in half-truths and more often lies. What did it matter to me if some corrupt city official had taken a back hander from the developer, and had kicked out all the former tenants, with their protected rents. What right did they have to live in such a great place for so little? This was a wealthy neighbourhood, and being wealthy should be the criteria for living here.

It was the second Friday of the month. I woke early to streams of sunlight flooding into the apartment. God what a sight, the mist hanging over the park, flocks of birds in the early morning sky, and not a single soul to disturb the majesty of it all.

I showered and then dressed in a crisp Armani suit, prepared for another exciting and financially rewarding day in court. I was defending a banker caught up in a Ponzi scheme worth many millions of dollars. Investors had lost everything, but one thing is for sure, the lawyer always gets paid. I locked the apartment door, and walked over to the elevator doors, pressing the down button. It opened at once; I must have been the last to use it the night before. I pressed 1 and the doors shut.

Caught up in my thoughts, I didn't notice at first that the elevator had stopped early on floor 6. As the doors opened I realised at once I wasn't on level one. The cool marble and glass of the entrance lobby were replaced by a filthy corridor, old paint work and builders rubble. I was on one of the unfinished floors. I jabbed 1 again, and the doors shut momentarily, before reopening again on floor 6. I pressed 1 again, no luck, then 13 – I thought I would go back to my apartment, but the elevator didn't budge.

I pressed the alarm button, and heard it ring, echoing, unanswered around the building. Typical shitty builders I thought. I'll take the stairs instead. I opened the door to the fire escape and took one step forward before realising, horrified, there were no steps. Where the concrete stairway should have been, was just an empty shaft six or seven storeys deep. I clung to the door, which swung out in to the chasm, before swinging me back to the hallway. I heard bits of dislodged concrete or plaster explode floors below me as they hurtled into the ground.

I knelt on the floor, knees and arms all dusty now, trembling and thankful for its solid presence beneath me. When I recovered my senses I stood and surveyed the corridor. Perhaps I could get to an external fire escape through one of the old apartments. The first door I approached was numbered 66 - 6. How cramped they must have been, compared to my spacious new home at the top.

I turned the handle and opened the door slowly, which gave way noisily into a dark dusty space. I could just about make out some light through blackened windows and drawn drapes. I searched around the wall for a light switch, my hand happening upon an unfamiliar switch, which I flicked down. At once a dim bulb without a shade flickered gloomily on, and off, on and off. It created unpleasant shadows around the room.

As the element in the light bulb warmed it settled down into a steady pale glow and I caught a sign of movement out of the corner of my eye. It took me by surprise, and filled me with new fears. Great, rats too! My eyes searched out for the movement, and fixed upon two filthy dirty, dusty piles of what looked like bandages, wrapped around child size forms.

One of them hissed quietly, "Please sir, don't hurt us," through an unseen mouth. As soon as it spoke I had to stifle a scream, which came out as a whimper. I called out, "Who are you? What are you doing here?"

A rasping voice replied, "We're the little boys, this is our home".

"Home? How do you live here?"

"Live Sir? We don't live".

I didn't comprehend what it said. "Who left you here?"

"The big boys, Sir. They have the dirty keys and move around the building as they want".

"Dirty keys?"

"Yes Sir, they travel between the walls and make their mischief".

I heard a distant scratching sound that in moments got louder.

"Please Sir, they're coming back, be a good little boy".

I sensed a dark, hollow, evil presence enter the room. It seemed to occupy every inch of the space, and a foul intoxicating smell filled my lungs. I was paralysed with fear, or something more real. My limbs were frozen, my eyes fixed as I felt the bandages being wrapped around me so tightly. I felt the very juices of my body, my blood, being drawn out of me. When it was over I was placed on the floor with the two other little boys, and we were left alone.

In the darkness of the room, we sometimes hiss words at each other, but for the most part of eternity we sit still, and quiet, like good little boys.

Safety First
Pat Burt

I couldn't put it off any longer - the toothache
was driving me mad. I found a local dentist,
checked with my police liaison officer - made an
appointment.

Life was so much easier now. The new me.
New name, new identity, new house in a new
location. So it should be after the three years of
misery and torment that bastard had put me
through. He meant nothing to me - just a guy at
work that I occasionally said "hallo" to. The
phone calls in the middle of the night. Dead
animals on my doorstep. Death threats through
the post. Why me - what had I done to deserve
it? Eventually they caught him and he was sent
to prison and I was given a new identity. Even
then I wasn't able to relax until the day I was told
he had died in prison.

And now that is all behind me - and I must get
to the dentist.

The waiting room was bright and cheerful; the
receptionist kind and sympathetic. Even the
magazines were up to date. A fish tank full of
brightly coloured fish added even more
tranquillity to a place that usually filled me full of
apprehension.

There were about four other patients waiting -
their noses stuck in books or magazines -
avoiding eye contact. Except for one man who
was fiddling with his iPad. He looked vaguely

familiar - but he had that kind of face. He looked up and smiled! Eventually I was called in. The dentist, an elderly man, gently prodded around.

"Sorry my dear, it's a root canal job. But we'll have to get that infection down before we can do anything. Hopefully we can save the tooth. You have very good teeth and have looked after them well. I'll give you some antibiotics and strong painkillers and we will see you again next week."

Clutching the prescription in my hand I noticed that the iPad man was still there. We nodded and I left to find a chemist.

The pain passed, the week passed, and it was time for my next appointment which was quite late in the afternoon. The iPad man was there again, the only other person waiting. He didn't look up. I was ushered in almost immediately.

"Ah yes, that's settled very nicely. I'll just give you a couple of injections to numb the gum so you won't feel any pain." I felt two or three strong pricks. "It will take a minute or two to take full effect."

With that I heard him go out the door. Minutes passed, the door opened.

"Hallo Maggie. Or is it Millie now?"

I tried to scream, to get out of the chair. Nothing.

"Sorry my dear, that injection made sure that you can neither move or make a sound. The wonders of modern medicine. You thought I was dead. So good of the police to tell you that. Only it wasn't the police. What a shame you didn't double check. Knowing people's weaknesses is a habit of mine. Money opens many doors. You see my dear - you can change your name, hair colour, even the colour of your eyes with contact lenses. I knew how fastidious you were about looking after your teeth - and the abscess came much sooner than anticipated. My spies soon found you - and the one thing you forgot to change was your dental records. So here I am and here you are - shall we get started?"

The Rival
Liz Tyrrell

Clare couldn't read maps. She held them upside down and confused left and right. She got tearful. Tom lost patience.

So Stella (the star) arrived. Fixed in the car, directing and advising. Never irritated, always reasonable.

"Take third exit." (Soft and patient.) "Keep straight ahead." (Unruffled.) "Recalculating!" (Serene.)

"Totally unnecessary!" Clare protested on routine journeys.

"That sexy voice," Tom explained. "She's indispensable. Keeps me company." A green light flashed. It wasn't a traffic signal. "Thought you'd got over being jealous," said Tom. "It's not worthy of you, darling."

"She sounds common to me!" Clare snarled. Get a grip, she told herself. Slow down! Just a machine, wasn't she? Some disembodied automaton. But she gloated when Stella mistook a nightclub for a hospital and mocked when she produced a word not heard before.

"Ferry!" jeered Clare, "Oh, I say!"

"Steady!" Tom cautioned. "You're losing it!"

"Bit of plastic!" jeered Clare. "Bet she wouldn't wash your socks!"

"Recalculating!" snapped Stella.

Driving alone one day, Clare needed help. A new district, an unfamiliar address. Stella was switched off. No response when Clare jabbed her, nor at the second vicious poke. Sulking? Missing Tom? Only at the third punch did she revive. Hostile. Harsh.

"Turn right, keep left!" What?

"Keep right, turn right!" Meaningless.

"Right, left, left, right!" Booming, deafening.

"Ping, exceeding-speed limit, PING!"

Clare pushed "Mute" with all her strength. Blessed silence. But then, "Enter tunnel!" Open countryside, no tunnel.

"Stella!" she pleaded. "I'm sorry! Please help me."

Stella softened. "At roundabout take the second exit!"

So far, so good.

"Straight ahead!" Manic again. "Straight ahead!" Getting louder. "First exit!"

Thundering…"First exit!"

Too late the one-way sign, alarmed faces, a brick wall….

"Arriving at destination," cooed Stella.

Retribution
Christine Maskell

Grace Moorland stood looking down at the inert form of her husband.

The blood had formed a pool on the kitchen floor, the bright red darkening as it cooled on the tiles. She recalled dropping a bottle of Shiraz once, her fingers stiff and painful after another "accident" with the rolling pin. The wine had found its way into the cracks between the tiles, like the blood. Her hand continued to clench the knife, protection in case he should suddenly find the strength to get up and attempt to hit her again.

The day had begun like any other; she got up an hour earlier than her husband, to prepare his breakfast. This necessitated walking to the village bakery to purchase freshly baked rolls each day, one for his lightly boiled eggs and two, suitably filled and placed on the right in his briefcase with a flask of coffee, to be enjoyed later, at the office. Today though, there had been a problem with the oven and no fresh rolls were available. She had been forced to buy a wholemeal loaf from the corner shop instead. It was raining, persistent rain from a gun metal sky, splashing against her legs as she walked. She was dreading the reaction her purchase would evoke. On her return home she put the water on for the eggs and went halfway upstairs to listen for sounds of Ken. He was already in the shower so she hurriedly laid out his Thursday suit, grey like the weather; matching socks and clean shirt. She was never allowed to choose the tie, he always did that. A small vanity, but she didn't mind, it probably saved her a few bruises.

Of course the bread was wrong, she knew it would be; which is why she was nervous and miscalculated the timing of the eggs. As Grace sliced the tops off, she realised they were slightly underdone, but it was too late to do anything different. She buttered and cut the bread into fingers and was putting the finishing touches to the sandwiches, when Ken came downstairs. He looked at the pale yellow yolks, he looked at the bread.

"You stupid bitch!" he yelled, making her cringe. "I can't eat this rubbish, you know I only eat a five minute egg; and where's my usual roll?"

In anger, he reached across to the stove and threw the saucepan at Grace. The metal pan hit her on the side of her head, the still hot water scalding her face, neck and chest. She gasped and in that instant a white heat overwhelmed her and she used all her strength to push him away. Of course the outcome would have been different if she weren't slicing a tomato with her favourite, very sharp knife, or indeed, if he had not been standing so close to her.

Instead, he had looked surprised as he staggered back, his pale blue eyes widening as he tried to lunge at her again.

"Now look what you've done, you stupid bitch!" he said, looking down at the dark stain spreading across his shirt. Grace said nothing, only watched as he slowly crumpled towards the floor. "Don't just stand there, bitch, call an ambulance!" he gasped.

But as if in a dream she watched as the stain increased, pooling under him and spreading across the tiles as his efforts to staunch it became more and more feeble. He looked at her, puzzled that his power to intimidate had failed, until eventually his eyes stared sightlessly up at the ceiling.

Mad March Hares
Richard Shakesheff

I caught a final glimpse of Hannah as the train pulled out of the station, her yellow dress and wide-brimmed hat as sunny as the day. In moments great plumes of steam and smoke obscured my view of her and she was gone. Soon the train had left Exmouth behind and the excitement I had felt in the days before gave way at once to a deep pang of regret and loss.

I had never travelled away from home and now without my sweetheart by my side I felt uncertain about the future. I was a willing volunteer to the Great War. I had signed up as soon as I could, along with dozens of my pals and work mates. No man or boy wanted to be left at home, a coward. Almost a year later, having spent endless days at drill practice with my pals I now found myself in France. In all that time I had sent my wages home, and so could not afford to take the train back to see Hannah when I was given a four day leave. Still, the war was supposed to be over soon, so it wouldn't be long before I was home. Instead I spent the time at the barracks polishing my boots and readying my kit. Now I was at war and wanted to get stuck in and do my bit.

I had placed a photo of Hannah in an old tobacco tin and had secured that in a button down breast pocket of my tunic. War was not the romantic adventure I had expected. The constant bombardments, day and night, the mud and ice, the ceaseless fear of death and of having to kill merged into one. I allowed myself one look at her picture a day. I did not want to sully her memory while all about lay death and horror. The rats at night, scurrying over my sleeping carcass, the lice that crawled on my skin and in my hair. It was not a place for

Hannah to be seen. The day I had been dreading came, when the whistle blew and we went over, running through no man's land, bullets and bombs flying everywhere. I fell into an unseen trench, off from the main enemy line and came across a boy or man about my age, squatting in the mud, trousers around his ankles, relieving the symptoms of dysentery. Our startled eyes met, both blue, and for a second the world seemed to stand still. Both him and me, confronted with our worse fears.

With both my hands and arms shaking I thrust my rifle forward at the man, its bayonet punching into his chest. The man fell back on to his behind, and into his own mess, arms outstretched, like a scolded child. A thick black-red ooze seeped from his chest. His eyes searching mine for any sign of humanity, but he found none.

I jabbed again, this time harder. Blood spurted out, hitting my face and turning my white teeth crimson.

As soon as it had begun it was over. A whistle sounded the retreat, and I scrambled out of the trench and scurried back to my own lines. In the melee my precious photo of Hannah, in its tin case, was lost. I knew it was my penance for the murderous act I had completed. In the safety of our own trench, I threw up and cried.

I had fired my rifle at the enemy plenty of times, but whether I hit anyone was another thing. Stabbing a man in cold blood was something different. It felt wrong, and I wondered about his sweetheart, waiting at home for his return, never to be.

The winter gave way briefly to spring, and with it hope. The shelling stopped and, after a few days of calm, I inched up a ladder in the trench to get a view of the battlefield. I saw to my bewilderment the mud and water had transformed into a sea of lush grass and flowers. It was a magical relief from the grime and muck. At once, in the middle of no man's land I saw two hares. They were sat on their hind quarters and seemed to be boxing each other, fighting over some unseen quarrel.

In the midst of all this passing beauty, two animals fighting. Is Mother Nature so cruel and senseless? Were we all just Mad March Hares fighting over a muddy field in a country foreign to all?

That night the shelling started again, and with it the winter returned. Icy wind brought heavy snow which melted into deep puddles in the trenches. My feet, constantly soaking wet through rotten boots, became numb and blistered with sores.

As time went on, one by one, the pals I joined with were killed, or horribly injured and taken to the rear. Bodies would lie stacked up in piles, awaiting burial, but the ground was too hard with frost. My pals were replaced with new cannon fodder; wide eyed, clean looking young men who very quickly lost their newness.

One night, my feet in terrible shape, I snuck along to the pile of bodies, and seeing one with a good pair of boots on, I stole them off the cold corpse, and replaced them with my own. A small young soldier saw me putting my old boots on the mangled dead feet. I looked at his startled face and said, "What are you looking at? He won't need them anymore."

Later I heard the young soldier crying to himself and calling out to his mother. I didn't pity him; I had nothing left in me. I closed my eyes and thought about Hannah, as I always did at night. I tried to remember her scent, but it was gone.

As days turned into weeks, and weeks to months, my nightly ritual of thinking about Hannah went on. But each day, little by little, I began to forget things about her. The colour of her hair, was it blonde or brown? Her face became blank, featureless. The loss of her memory was more than I could bear. I sat staring into space, like all the other old timers, boys really, but ones who had suffered the longest in the trenches. My mind devoid of all thought, immune now to the barrages and bullets. Nothing mattered.

The whistle blew again, and we all climbed up the ladders and ran at the enemy.

The Listener
Pat Burt

Oh no, not her!

I cannot see, but I can hear and feel and I think this one coming towards me must have done her initial training at Guantanamo Bay. She certainly took her blood-letting exams with Dyna Rod. I just hope it isn't time to change the catheter.

More footsteps. Visitors. My oh-so-worried son and his equally caring wife. Worried that I might recover! Believe me sunshine, I am going to recover, just to see the look on your faces when I tell you that I could hear everything. And as for you Nurse whoever you are, there's going to be a lovely little report about you.

"How is she today?" Here we go.

"No change. We're making her as comfortable as possible."

Footsteps receding. That Nurse is so heavy on her feet the ward trembles.

"Not worth staying here, nothing we can do. Don't forget the Estate Agent's coming round to look at her house."

"It doesn't seem right, valuing her property. She isn't dead."

"May as well be. We've got to start getting things sorted before your sister starts butting in. You're the oldest."

So that's her little game, the scheming minx. We'll see about that.

"At least we could start sorting out her belongings. Her jewellery for instance – she's got a few nice pieces. Get in there first I say."

"No Angelina – I couldn't."

"You're such a wimp. Anyway we are only taking what will soon be ours. If we don't, your sister and her brats will."

Are you so thick that you haven't heard of such things as a will? But I shouldn't let it bother you because I am going to recover. If I could just blink – waggle a finger. Concentrate girl – come on, you can do it.

"Can't we go? You know I hate hanging around this morbid dump."

"Not yet. They said we had to talk to her or play some music. Well I downloaded some of her favourites onto this iPod. I'll just set it up for her."

"You idiot – wasting more money. It'll get stolen as soon as our backs are turned, just you see."

"I doubt it. It's worth a try."

Whatever made him think I liked R.E.M.? That's enough to push me right over the top. Come on, twitch, girl. Twitch.

"Look – her mouth is moving!"

"Rubbish, it's just wind."

"No, no look! Her hand, the fingers, they are twitching – I'm going to fetch the Nurse."

Good boy! Footsteps running. By the time you get back I'll be sitting up in bed singing.

"You're not going to recover. I'm going to make sure of that!"

67

What's that on my face? I can't breathe.
    "Angelica! What are you doing with that pillow? Throw it on the floor." I hear myself screaming.

It Is Always the Same Dream
Christine Maskell

To begin with, it is light and I am walking down a long road – I am alone and there is no sound. On either side are trees, bare branches curling and stretching down towards the road, like gnarled fingers. At first, I smile at such fanciful thoughts, but as I walk, the silence becomes dark, depressive, and ominous and, although there is no sound, I feel as though I am being followed.

    The tree trunks slowly develop elongated faces that frown at me, or have angry open mouths and their branches reach out towards me as though to clutch at me and drag me who knows where. The road here narrows and I begin to feel the fear clutching at my stomach.

    I hurry, but the ribbon of road stretches endlessly in front of me. I have no idea where I am headed and the light begins to fade, imperceptibly at first until suddenly, I am surrounded by full darkness. My back begins to prickle but I know I mustn't look around, because, if I do, whatever is out there, will devour me. I start to run but, as I do, the ribbon of road turns to mud, mud which sucks at my feet, slowing me down, threatening to swallow me. My heart is thumping now, I can feel the sweat running cold down my back and I anticipate cold bony fingers digging into my flesh. I force myself to try and run faster through the glutinous path, and my heart is beating ever faster.

Suddenly, because until now I haven't seen it, a building appears and there is a staircase on the outside of it, spiralling up and up. I grasp the rail thankfully, glad to free myself from the slimy morass and begin to climb. How much longer can I do this, my leg muscles ache, my heart is pounding so hard it threatens to burst from my chest, yet still I feel as though some creature is only a few steps behind me, about to grasp my hair and yank me back down into the slime.

Suddenly, I am on the roof, the staircase has disappeared and the only way forward is to jump. I cannot. I am more afraid of heights than of any creature that may consume me. I stand precariously balanced on the very edge, feeling giddy, with my stomach turning somersaults and a little voice whispering, "Go on! Jump!" The fear I feel is very real, but, even so, I prefer to face whatever it is behind me, than jump off the roof.

I turn slowly around to face my tormentor and wake, heart pounding still, wet with sweat, remembering only the feeling of fear. Fumbling, I put on the light and I'm in my room, where everything is normal. I dare not sleep again for fear that whatever is waiting for me in the dark hours, is still lurking.

When the Bookworm Turns
Liz Tyrrell

I'm feeling very excited today. I'm going to meet
Raymond - and his books - for the first time.

I spend a long time getting ready, trying to
look as much as possible like the photo I put
online, fluffing up my hair and being generous
with the lipstick. I've covered all the grey with
'Raven Princess'. Five years, well, ten maybe,
haven't really made much difference.

I'm taking Raymond a book as a present, the
obvious gift. It's one of my own, actually *Death
and the Dog-walker*. I can certainly spare it –
there are still three boxes of them in the garage.
Spent a good part of Gran's legacy on getting
them published. 'Vanity Publishing,' sniffed my
ex. I prefer 'Self-publishing'.

I know they say you should *rendezvous* in a
neutral place the first time you meet in the flesh,
but the thought of seeing all those books was too
good an opportunity to miss. Bibliophiles – that's
what we are, kindred spirits. I'm a big girl; I can
take care of myself.

That was what attracted me in the first place,
the way he talked about his books. Just the way
I feel. It's as if he derives nourishment from
them. He 'devours' novels, he 'relishes' and
'savours' poetry, once he's finished one thriller
he's 'hungry' for the next. He can never get
enough - like me he can't pass a bookshop
without buying - and good reviews 'whet his

appetite'. Kindle, of course, is a dirty word. No glossy cover to stroke, no pages to flick through. Although we both agree that using a turned-down page as a bookmark is violation of the worse kind.

"I know we'll get on", he posted enthusiastically. "My sort of people are always buried in books."

The house is two bus rides away. Off the beaten track and darkly secluded behind a screen of overgrown bushes. When he opens the door - with difficulty, it seems - I have a slight flicker of disappointment. He hasn't bothered to shave or, if he did, it was a very ancient razor. A faded shirt that needs an iron. Twenty years older than his online picture. I'm probably about the same age, but I don't look it.

I *was* attracted by the picture, I must admit.

Raymond was posing with an intensive look, paperback in hand, in front of neat rows of books and, when I zoomed in on them, I was excited to find we shared many titles. Classics, short stories, biographies. I couldn't help but visualise the size of our eventual library because, of course, we're made for each other.

What do looks matter? Ours is a meeting of true minds.

It was so refreshing to meet someone whose intellect matched my own. I met very few prospective matches in that category and those I approached weren't interested. Perhaps the photo was too glamorous.

"Sylvia?"

He bows over my hand in an old-fashioned way.

"Raymond!"

The door only opens partway, impeded, I realise, by the tottering piles of precariously balanced books leaning against it. Too quickly, it closes behind me. He makes me go in front of him down a narrow pathway between slithering mountains of paperbacks and hardbacks, in no apparent order. Where are the neat shelves of the picture? A quick glance into the front room reveals more of the same, how can he find anything in this mess? Magazines fight with tatty encyclopaedias for floor space, ancient soft-backs obscure the windows. You couldn't put a pin between them and there's no discernible system. Mine are pristine, organised on spotless shelves by subject and author. It's even hard to make out any furniture in the room.

"I'll make some tea!" Raymond says leading me into what I imagine is the kitchen. Books press in from every side, a fire hazard, surely. I slide and nearly fall on an ancient copy of *Good Housekeeping*. I spot a filthy Baby Belling amid the chaos and decline the offer.

"I don't think so!" Raymond grabs me tightly round the wrist. I glance wildly about, no sign of a door, no sign of anything but books. There's an odd smell in here, I catch a glimpse of material that could be a woman's dress in a tottering mound where the back door should be.

"As I said", Raymond grins. "I like the kind of people who get buried in books."

Moving on
Michael Forrer

It's nice here. We had donuts and I like donuts. My friend had a donut too. She is my best friend ever. And I don't want to move house, I really don't. Mummy and Daddy showed me the new house and how nice it is and that Daddy has to move because of his job and that. It does have a big garden. But I want to stay here with my friend because her Mummy says she can't come with us.

Phoebe is in the same class as me. And we both looked after Jimmy the Gerbil but he died last week. Our teacher, Miss Weeks, told us off because we had put red powder paint in the water to see if he would turn pink. And just after school I walked back to the class and called Mrs Weeks bad names because I was sad and I did not mean to hurt Jimmy. Mrs Weeks was shocked. I thought she was going to hit me when she raised her hand to slap me. But she stopped. And I cried. And Mrs Weeks gave me a handkerchief and put her arm around me and told me she would not be cross about the gerbil dying but that we must think before we do things because sometimes we can hurt people without realizing it.

I forgot. You don't know who I am. I'm Zara. Means princess, and that's what Daddy calls me.

I have a little brother called Gregory, but he is too small to even speak. I love it when he giggles when I make faces. I love Christmas too. I want a puppy for Christmas. I am going to be a real princess when I grow up.

What else can I tell you about me? I get frightened sometimes. Not when my Daddy pretends to scare me. But when Mr Robbins walks past our house. He has glasses and is always looking at his boots. He walks funny, like he is stamping on a spider each time he puts his foot down. Mr Robbins walks past our house every day – I don't know where he goes. He lives on his own in the house up the road. Daddy says it is a disgrace because the paint is peeling and his garden is replacing the rainforests. He used to have children once and their mummy. But now he is on his own and no one goes to the house except the postman. One day I was in our front garden and Mr Robbins walked past. I said hello and he just went, "Go away. Go away." He just walked on, pretending to kill spiders.

My friend Phoebe is really brave. She jumped across the stream in the woods even though I screamed at her not too. I thought she would fall and bang her head or drown or something and I wouldn't know what to do. But she just jumped and turned around and laughed out loud so that I had to laugh too.

Phoebe and I have a secret. Don't tell anyone will you? It was Phoebe's idea and I said yes, even though I'm scared. Phoebe says we should go and explore Mr Robbins' garden, and that if it's like a rainforest she thinks there might be some animals there that no one knows about.

So we are going tomorrow after school. I might tell Mummy I am going to Phoebe's house next door, because I am. Good night - I am going to sleep now.

oOo

I thought about it all day at school. And now we are nearly at Mr Robbins house, Phoebe and me. At the corner of the street. A piece of wood in his fence is missing so Phoebe peers in, and climbs through sideways. I am a bit bigger than her and have to twist the next piece of wood and squeeze much more. "Come on, Zara, quickly,"' she says, as I just manage to get through. 'Ow!' says Phoebe as she climbs through the brambles. But I keep on following. The grass is high and wet, covered in jewels where the sun is shining.

There is a path made of red bricks. I step on to it – Phoebe's seen it too. She jumps out of the grass on to the path. I sort of scream. A loud scream inside but no noise outside. Something's splashed all over my legs. Brown splodges everywhere. Even Phoebe looks a bit upset.

"I jumped on a great big brown slug and it burst," she says to me. I wanted to cry but was too frightened. "Phoebe, why did you do that?" Phoebe looks straight at me. "It didn't see me coming," she says.

We move away from the slimy mess towards an old shed further into the garden. We can hardly see Mr Robbins' house, there are so many big bushes. So he can't see us and I am less scared. Zara, be a brave girl, I tell myself when the cobwebs stretch and break as we open the old wooden door. It is dark inside the shed. There are no windows. Spiders can be quite nice really, can't they? I watched one in our garden. When I touched its web with a bit of leaf, out it came, as if to say Hello, Zara.

Inside the shed is very big, and thin bits of light shine through the cracks in the wood so we can see the spades and forks and a big saw hanging on the wall. And the longer we stay the less dark it gets. It's our place, our hidey place. There is a big red and green machine with a great big metal roller thing. It smells funny, like when Mummy puts petrol into our car to make it go further.

And there is a wooden bench, we stretch up to see on to. It's very dirty and cobwebby. And I think I can see a spider hiding at the edge. It moved, I think. I try looking again from the corner of my eye, because it won't move if it knows I'm looking. I can see its big shiny round body, and for a moment I just look at it and wonder if it is looking at me. It just stays there on tiptoes.

"Zara, what's this?" asks Phoebe. I am surprised she doesn't know. My uncle has one and holds it between his teeth for ages. I have never seen one anywhere else. He sucks it and makes it glow and then blows out the smoke. Mummy says it is a disgusting habit.

"It's a pipe, of course." I'm pleased to know something Phoebe doesn't. "You need matches to make it work."

"Here are the matches," says Phoebe.

Phoebe holds the box in her hand and pushes the little cardboard drawer open with the longest finger of her other hand. The little red heads lie there cosily, like lots of little wooden people sleeping in the same cot. She doesn't say anything as she gets one out, but we are both looking at the match and forgetting about spiders, or slugs, or Mr Robbins. "You slide the red bit down the edge," I hear myself saying.

"I know that!" says Phoebe, as if she really does. She scrapes the wooden little stick down and makes a crackling sound against the edge. We see tiny sparks explode into a flame. It's only a small flame, but it fills our eyes as if we had discovered something from another world. It flickers for a few seconds. Then Phoebe has to let go. It is too hot. And the burning match falls to the floor.

Somehow we have scared ourselves so much that we rush for the door. I trip over the wooden step and land face down in the wet grass and Phoebe jumps over me. It hurts a bit, but I am not going to show it.

I can see his house now, or part of it. One upstairs window with the curtain closed. It does need painting. Perhaps we could paint it for him if he wasn't so scary. Phoebe gives me a friendly push. "Come on," she says. And we don't even notice the dark grey rat peering out from the wire netting which holds together an old compost heap. But the rat sees us with its little beady pink eyes. Its whiskers are twitching at the unfamiliar smell of small children and are instinctively alert to the trace of smoke in the air.

I see the rat first as it scurries away under the compost and that's when *it* jumps out of the bushes. So fast, so big. It grabs me and lifts me up and runs. So fast that I think I am going to fall.

And then the warmth comes and the brightness. Like the sun has exploded and its fiery arms have reached out to burn us. And the monster falls to the ground and I fall with him on to the wet grass. I think I hear screams.

I turn, confused, to see the monster's fearful face – with horrible dark black bushy overgrown eyebrows looking like they had been stuck on to a Mr Potato-head. And beneath them, two panes of glass, eye windows, and in them I see the reflection of the orange flames pouring from the shed. And I can't see Phoebe.

I never see Phoebe now.

Someone said she was just in my head, my imagination. I knew she was real to me. And we moved house, and I like the garden and Daddy is going to make me a little wooden house at the end of the garden just for me and my friends.

We don't talk about Phoebe.

But we do go back sometimes. To see Mr Robbins. We even have tea in his house. He was in hospital for a while. But he says he is happy to see us. Says he was so pleased to have seen it and been just in time, this time. And then he looks a bit sad before cheering up and saying, "It makes life worth living again."

Mr Robbins is a best friend now. He showed me a great big frog in the pond in his garden, last time we were there. 'Handsome' he said it was.

But I never forget Phoebe.

Another Sussex Murder Story
by The B(est) Team
aka Jan Thompson, Julie Gibbons, Liz Carboni, Liz Tyrell, Michael Forrer, Sallie A Sawicka and Bridget Whelan

The Husband

Each time I pick it up I admire it: the dark brown rosewood between the frets, the curves of its body - so carefully hand-crafted. A classical guitar bought near Madrid during that holiday with Suzy when we had done such crazy stuff. I found it at a workshop that has made guitars for generations. We both knew I couldn't afford it - but she laughed and encouraged me. So I bought it anyway. And sixteen years later, that's one decision without regret.

It's still as beautiful as the day I bought it. In such a different class to the guitars I learnt to play on, starting with a gift on my sixth birthday - a toy plastic guitar with four nylon strings and a hidden musical box that played *Oh Susannah* when you turned a handle at the side.

Work and music fill most of my time outside home. Work to pay the bills and music with the band that calls itself professional but doesn't earn enough to keep one of us, let alone six musicians and their families. It just about paid for my season ticket to watch the Seagulls' home games. And the petrol for taxiing Robert to wherever he wants to go. Thirteen years old already. At first I didn't really want any children and neither had Suzy. But Robert decided to arrive, and he suits us and I think we suit him.

I strummed *Oh Susannah* very quietly, my fingers almost floating over the strings.

"Steve, don't you need to go to rehearsal?" Suzy's shouting from the bottom of the stairs, as she does every Tuesday evening. She's right; I must go soon. The rest of the band likes starting on time and next week we have a gig in Chichester.

I carefully put the guitar back into its black felt-lined case, carried it downstairs and called out goodbye to Suzy who was busy on her laptop preparing for some work meeting tomorrow.

Now it was my turn to shout upstairs: "Bye, Robert". And I was lucky this time to get a response - an increase in the volume of the music piercing his bedroom door.

I drove through Ardingly still remembering that Spanish holiday, turned right and continued, half dreaming, half driving to Haywards Heath, looking forward to seeing the band in the practice studio we hired; a converted old chapel on the edge of town. When I pushed open the heavy door I saw that everyone was setting up except Paul, our new vocalist. Paul drove a taxi for a living and told us that sometimes he would be late. With that baritone voice, it seemed worth taking the risk.

The Lover

I met her at the gym. I'd never been able to afford to go to one before, not even the council one at the King Alfred. But £11 million changes a lot of things. You might have read about it. The Argus splashed it on the front page when I won the lottery.

I bought a luxury seafront flat. A penthouse the estate agent called it. Now I'm kitted out head to toe in Ted Baker and have a Mercedes sports car - top of the range - parked in my garage. I joined a country club and driving out there most days gave me something to do. I booked a personal trainer. I'd had a pretty tough time before this and my self-confidence was rock bottom. My Mum never cared about me - threw me out of the house to make way for her then boyfriend. So all this money was a great boost to my esteem. The only thing missing in my life was a woman.

Suzy had the same personal trainer. Her slot was after mine. She was gorgeous, just my type, quite a few years older than me, well rounded and pretty.

That first time I hung around and then offered her a coffee. We got on really well and arranged to meet after her next session. Things developed quickly. She would come back to the flat after her training, and we soon conjured up a friend who she would pretend to meet in the evening, sometimes for a drink and dinner. She became my lover, friend and confidante and I was soon obsessed with planning a future together. The fact that she was married with a son didn't concern me. I needed her, just like I needed the flat and the car and the fancy clothes.

The Son

I knew there was something wrong between Mum and Dad. Not that they argued. It was the silences and the forced politeness that was the giveaway. That particular night Dad went out straight after supper. He's a musician, and meets up with mates to rehearse for gigs. Personally, I think it's more of a booze up, but he enjoys himself.

Well, Dad had barely reversed out of the drive when Mum came into the lounge. She was breathless and a bit flushed.

"Just off to see my friend. Best not to mention it to Dad."

She slammed out of the door before I could reply. Living out in the sticks means that the buses are rubbish and I knew she had to rush to catch the next one. Then I was left thinking, why bother to change into a short dress and put on half a ton of perfume to meet a girlfriend? Of course she's got another man. Come to think of it I'd heard her whispering on the phone, and she had a funny look on her face when she came back in the room. I can always tell when she's lying.

Poor Dad. But if they do split up what will happen to me? Will I have to choose between them?

It's dark outside now. I wonder what Mum's doing and where she is. I dialled her mobile. It rang and rang and I thought it was going to her usual lame answerphone message and then I heard her voice.

"Robbie, what's wrong?"

I did the best impression of a sick person I could. Really, I deserved an Oscar. I could hear the panic in her voice.

"Don't worry, I'm coming straight home."

As her phone clicked off I started to feel a bit guilty but I wanted her home.

The Taxi Driver

Why we had to move to Sussex I shall never know; a fresh start, a new life, clean air and a greener future she said.

In London I was just another mini cab driver with a Satnav who never got the hang of the North Circular. Green Lanes was green enough for me, and the salad in my free kebabs counted as my five a day. Down here I have a cab license and I am a bit of a looker compared to the grey haired old timers. We've rented a house in Peacehaven with a garden; the wife loves the garden, the weird bloke next door is giving her hints about English flowers. Perhaps she has found her Peace Haven?

It's raining tonight which is always good for the moneybag. Thought I'd put in a couple of hours in Brighton and then I'd make my way over to Haywards Heath for band practice. She doesn't know about that. I don't tell her everything.

The shift started badly when the weirdo from next door begged a lift into Brighton. I am sure she puts him up to it, he's a preacher and, according to her, I need God in my life with a bit of Jesus on the side. Sad git, wife left him, kid dead, real loser. As usual he asks about the women I pick up late at night, "Are they all prostitutes?" he lisps. I explain, in slightly exaggerated terms, that they are not all like that. Some are just young women who are pleased to see a handsome Latino guy willing to forgo the full fare! I laugh and turn to look at his face, he coughs and slobbers slightly and his eyes are on stalks.

"So, neighbour, where shall I drop you tonight?"

"Oh, anywhere near the Level," he says restraining his excitement. In his rush he drops his bag in the gutter.

"I'll get it, stand still." I beat him to it and hand it over. "Wow! That's heavy," I say.

"The word of God," he mutters.

I kerb crawl a couple of bus stops, ignoring a pair of old ladies waving their bingo wings, not tonight darlings, all that talk with Holy Joe has had its effect! I look at this one in the rear view mirrors; nice, wet, but nice.

"In you get lady!"

No reply. I see she is crying, not sad, more frustrated angry. She's perfect: a long fare out into the country. I can drop her off and still get the Haywards Heath to join the band for the last hour. Unless she's up for something.

"Want to talk about it?" I ooze sympathy. I ooze Mr Nice.

She was crying hard, but lets out her story between sobs and at first doesn't notice when I pull over near The Level. I study her in the rear view mirror and can see she's older than I thought, a little tarty in that short wet dress. My face holds no secrets, and she can see exactly what I am about as I slip in the back seat.

"Bloody men, you just never get it right do you?"

"Whoa, lady! Ok, I'll take you home." I tell her. I mean it too, because now I am up close I recognise her and don't want any trouble.

"Don't bother!"

I watch as she walks off towards The Level. Did she recognise me I wonder; I've seen her before at a gig a few weeks ago. She didn't look like she did tonight, more jeans and a cardi then, and all over Steve, blowing kisses; all little wifey. Might be worth going after her, calm her down a bit, perhaps she'll be a bit more friendly when she knows how well I know her husband. She'll want to keep me quiet, after all Steve might find out what she's been up to.

The Wife

It's so dark. Where am I? Piles of earth, machinery. Oh I know. The Level. That's where I am. But where are the paths? If I can cross The Level I'll be able to catch a bus in London Road. But I can't see where I am going. It's all dug up. I remember now. They are re-designing it. The whole area. They must have left some paths though. And lights. I'm sure there were lights in this place. They can't have taken them all down. I've got to be careful or I'll trip with all these mud heaps and holes. Which way do I go now? I'm going to ring Mr Champagne – he can come and pick me up.

If it wasn't raining so hard perhaps I could see better. No answer. Where could he be? I wonder if he's followed me. He's done that before. No, I bet he's sulking. If he doesn't get his own way he becomes a different man, demanding, calculating, even a bit cruel. This is to punish me for going home to my son.

I wonder if that awful taxi driver is still around. I don't want to meet up with him again. Should be able to see the lights of Ditchling Road by now and I can't. Have I been going round and round in the dark? That's what they say you do. This is ridiculous I'm in the centre of town and bloody lost.

Still no answer from lover boy. Better stop and have a good look round. Didn't I see that bulldozer thing a few minutes ago? I'm sure I did. Wait, there's a faint haze of lights behind me. Is that the road I have just left or the road I'm trying to get to? I'm so confused. And wet. And cold.

I can see someone coming. Is it the horrible taxi driver? Whoever it is he is carrying a bag. And he's hurrying. I'll speak to him. He'll put me on the right path, I hope. Only I don't know. There's something about the way he's running towards me that makes me scared, like I'm a target and he's an arrow.

The Neighbour

I've made it my mission in life - saving fallen women. From themselves really. If they knew how vulnerable they are running around after midnight dressed in next to nothing and full of booze. Just asking for trouble.

It's because of my wife that I'm able to do it. We lost our little girl when she was five years old and she never got over it. "Just think," she'd say as another teenager crashed into the gutter totally out of her head, "that could have been our Rosie." I resist the temptation to say that maybe the meningitis was for the best if it spared her from degradation like this.

It was the wife's idea to join The Street Angels. Every Friday and Saturday night we'd drive into the city centre, put on our badges and look for those in need. She had a real flair for it, but somehow the church that organised it weren't keen on my approach.

"You shouldn't wave the bible at them!" Father Tim would say. "That's not what they need right now."

I didn't agree, of course, but Father Tim was obviously keeping tabs on us with the result that, one night, I was told not to come anymore. Imagine - giving up our time, volunteering from the goodness of our hearts and you're expelled like some naughty schoolboy.

They still wanted the wife, though. We rowed about it later; she accused me of all sorts of things. It was when she started on the old tack of

not calling the doctor quickly enough for Rosie -
"God will provide, you said!" - that I really saw
red. Hadn't realised the Holy Book would make
such a mess of her face. Her own fault. That's
when she moved out.

I don't mind living alone. The neighbours are
very good. I go out alone now. I pinched the
wife's badge and stick to the back streets around
London Road. I like the shadows around The
Level. I can hear a woman running. Running to
salvation.

The Lover

The police questioned me, of course, and I had
to make a statement. I told them the truth.

The evening was going to be special. I'd
organised an elaborate meal with lots of
champagne. I'd bought her a present; a diamond
necklace which would be kept in my safe, to be
worn only for me. I didn't get a chance to give it
to her. The night started well. We sipped
champagne whilst the meal was cooking and
she showed off her newly toned body. We made
love. Then things changed... I said I wanted her
to leave her husband and son and move in with
me. She said she wasn't ready. She was
frightened. I tried to persuade her.

She seemed to be listening but then her
mobile phone rang. It was her son, Robbie, a
boy who suffered with his nerves. Whined, said

he was ill, made a fuss. He begged her to come home.

"Of course, sweetie," she said.

I was so angry. I smashed a glass of champagne against the wall and shouted something about wasting my time and money on her. I may have called her a selfish bitch, I don't remember. But I do remember Suzy rushing out and slamming the door.

I followed but the elevator doors were already closed. From my window I watched her walking up the street towards a taxi rank.

Later I had a missed call from her. I'd been in the shower. ("Was I showering to wash away the evidence?" the police asked. "Did I return the call and arrange to meet her?") I tried ringing back, again and again, but I only got her answerphone. No, I didn't leave a message.

No one's been arrested yet. I've put up a substantial reward for information you know. I don't care about money now. It means nothing to me. There's an empty space in my heart that was once filled by Suzy. I like to think she was calling to say that she was coming back to me, leaving her family. That I was the only person she wanted to be with. This is what I believe. This is what I tell myself. It comforts me.

It wasn't meant to end like this. Suzy, sweet vulnerable Suzy. If we hadn't quarrelled. If she hadn't made me so mad…If her son hadn't rung…

They found her on The Level the next morning.

Poor Suzy. Quite dead.

Where Did That Come From….?

The Sussex Murder Mystery A and B

Bridget says: I read an article about a co-operative writing exercise dealing with a murder of an adulterous wife written from various points of view to explore who was really guilty. I adapted the idea, divided the class into two and handed out the assigned parts at random. Once Portslade Penpushers had shared what they had written they could discuss how the plot was evolving and agree on the story line and re-write as necessary.

Sounds simple, doesn't it? It wasn't.

The writers weren't the problem. They did a grand job and there was even-handed negotiation and compromise within the writing teams. And a lot of laughter. And it didn't matter that somehow the rebels in Group B created a new character – the sinister neighbour. I caused the problem when I attached the Group A husband to the Group B wife. I've given myself a writing credit on both stories because it took a lot of imagination to get out of that hole.

The Street Singer
Sallie says: the plight of the homeless and mentally ill is so often ignored.

The Old Tenement Block
Richard says: this horror story about the big boys and the dirty keys came to me in a dream (too much cheese!)

Safety First
Pat says: I've no idea where this came from – somewhere in the depths!

The Rival
Liz says: my partner has a Sat Nav, also named Stella, about which we joke and fantasise but it has never gone this far!

Retribution
Christine says: it stemmed from a newspaper article concerning battered women. I took it a step further.

Mad March Hares
Richard says: the story grew out of a class

exercise when Bridget brought in a number of objects including an old chipped mug celebrating the end of the Great War. I wrote it to submit for a competition with the same title that Bridget told us about. I never got round to submitting it.

The Listener
Pat says: I got the idea after watching a TV report on euthanasia.

It's Always the Same Dream
Christine says: I hate heights and this is a recurring nightmare.

When the Bookworm Turns
Liz says: the phrase 'to be buried in a book' occurred to me and I worked towards that.

Moving on
Michael says: Bridget asked us to write from the point of view of a child, and so Zara and her friend Phoebe were born….

SLOW, SLOW

And by the way, everything in life is writeable about if you have the outgoing guts to do it, and the imagination to improvise. The worst enemy to creativity is self-doubt. Sylvia Plath

In and Out
Hélène Meredith

Summer Loving
Julie Gibbons

Hove Beach
João Sousa

A High and Endless Summer - Brighton June '73
Charlie Bowker

The Red Dungarees
Hélène Meredith

Hooked On Crochet
Julie Gibbons

The Pond
Christine Maskell

A Raven Wept
Janis Thomson

The Potato Peeler
Christine Maskell

In and Out

Hélène Meredith

Into this space I shall leave
My right arm,
A hollow tube of metal filled with lead,
My hair,
A depleted scarecrow,
My forgetfulness,
A cloud surrounding my brain.
Love handles,
Something I do not love and can't handle.
Cleaning,
An endless, repetitive, tiring exercise.
(Could someone do it for me, please?)
Long car journeys,
A claustrophobic and tedious way
To see the world.
Out of this space I shall take
A world without pain,
My hair before chemo,
A sharp mind and slender body,
A magic wand to clean
And a flying carpet to travel.

Summer Loving
Julie Gibbons

Summer was 15 when she first fell in love. Quite old compared with other girls, but then, she wasn't like other girls in her class. Taller, larger, slower. She would like to have been different in many ways. To have straight hair like Amy, or to be skinny, like Michelle.

She hated her name too. It was ridiculous and embarrassing. Her parents, much as she loved them, had never lost their hippy looks. For goodness sake, they were in their forties. Her mother still wore kaftans and her father would have looked years younger without his long beard. Their home was shabby chic, with more of an emphasis on the shabby.

A daydreamer, it had never occurred to her to get work in the long summer holidays. She'd been looking forward to messing around with her friends, going to the shops, the cinema. Her mother had given her little choice.

"They need help in the teashop. I said you'd be happy to lend a hand."

Put like that refusal wasn't an option.

So, on the first Saturday in August, Summer presented herself at The Toasted Teacake. It was a cramped and busy little shop. Summer felt as if she was entering a doll's house. Another girl standing behind the counter gave a nod and a grunt, and Mrs. Rivers, the manageress, hurried forward.

"Thank goodness you're here dear. One of the waitresses has let me down. Now come through here."

She led Summer into a small back room.

"Here's your uniform."

Summer could tell at a glance it wasn't long enough for her. She looked with dismay at the pale blue dress and little white apron.

"Don't worry." Mrs. Rivers had misinterpreted Summer's expression as anxiety over the job.

"Just jot down the orders on this notepad and put it through the hatch."

Summer shuffled shyly into the teashop, desperately trying to pull down the dress. Most of the customers were steadily eating their way through a variety of dainty cakes and scones. As far as she could see there was only one person waiting to be served. He was sitting, with his back to her, on the far side of the café. She edged past the tables until she was close to him. Her stomach did a little flip as she saw the way his auburn hair curled at his neck. Flustered, she asked for his order.

"Just a coffee and a piece of chocolate cake, please."

Summer could hardly get the pen to write she was shaking so much, partly from nerves but mainly because of him. She edged back to the counter. Wow! What was the matter with her? A few minutes later she delivered his order.

He smiled up at her. "Great. You're new here aren't you?"

Blushing furiously, she could only nod in reply.

For the rest of the afternoon, long after he'd gone, she replayed those words in her mind. He wasn't like the spotty, silly boys at school who thought calling her lanky was funny. He was a mature man. Gosh, he must be at least 30.

The following day, she got up a little earlier. She decided to put on a small amount of make-up, and spend time getting her hair under control. She almost skipped along. Please, please God, let him be there today. Let me speak to him. I'll be good for the rest of the year. About 4 o'clock her wish came true. He sat in the same seat. She was about to rush over and take the order, but the manageress was there first.

"Ah, there you are, George. Same as usual?"

George. Wasn't that the best name in the world? George and Summer, Summer and George. She was so busy daydreaming that at first she didn't hear Mrs. Rivers calling her name.

"Hurry up, Summer, clear the tables please."

George left soon after, but not before he'd waved to her. When she got home, she locked herself into her bedroom and spent ages playing back in her mind everything she knew about him. She bought a pretty notebook. Inside, in her best writing, she wrote George, and surrounded it with a heart. Then she wrote down; Coffee, black, strong, three sugar lumps. Chocolate cake. Underneath that she wrote a description of him. Medium height, green eyes, auburn hair curling at nape of neck. Not very fashion-conscious, but she'd be able to alter that. On the next page, she jotted down everything he'd said to her, which, to date wasn't very much at all. Nevertheless, it all added up as the time went by.

Summer only worked three mornings a week although she would willingly have worked more. Most of the time she went around in a daze. Her notebook gradually filled up with snippets of chat with George. She always included what he was wearing. He looked especially good in a pale green sweater. She vowed to work extra hard at school after George told her how important education was.

Three weeks later everything changed. She was clearing tables when the bell rang to say there was a customer. Ah, George. But he was not alone. A small, pretty lady followed him. They were laughing and hugging and admiring the large diamond ring on her finger. Mrs. Rivers was by their side in an instant fussing over them. From behind the counter, Summer watched the scene. George would not be hers. He belonged to this tiny, perfect beauty.

When she got home, she fled to her bedroom and wept for hours.

She kept the pretty book with details of George for several years. Sometimes, she saw him with his wife around the town.

Gradually, Summer stopped thinking about him, but she never forgot the first time she fell in love.

Hove Beach

João Sousa

Waves in doubt
Lick gentle the shore

Green, the water
Breaks into folders of foam
And return, uncertain
Into the large mass
That looms into the horizon

Thoughts and doubts
Swept by the breeze;
Sparks of sunlight
Sprinkle the rugged water:
Stars descending into earth

Thin clouds now veil the blue.
A sail searches fortune.
The fish hide. They count
The waiting hours by the tide,
Swirl forth and back.
The water a net
To catch and swallow
 Incautious divers

The sun watches undisturbed

Water and sand,
Birds or tourists.
Winter and summer,
Night or day,

Life runs,
Life stays.

A High and Endless Summer - Brighton June 73

Charlie Bowker

The train from Victoria powered through the early evening, determined to get all those tired and sweaty bodies, baked and caked in the unpleasant city heat grime, home to their cooler south coast hideaways. The sun blazed in the sky.

Many of Dave's fellow passengers were long-haired hippies or students moving back from London squats to their communal homes by the sea. Badges exhorting *make love not war* could be seen emblazoned in flowers on some dresses, or stitched into kaftans. A guitar and the record sleeve of Pink Floyd's *Dark Side of the Moon* were visible amongst the brightly decorated bags and rucksacks filling the aisles and luggage racks. The smell of patchouli oil and dope hung around the carriages, annoying the sharp-suited accountants returning home to comfortable conservatism.

Dave emerged at the front of Brighton's Victorian station, laced with heady doses of sea air and generations of memories of exuberant seaside relationships. Where was this woman who had so captured his imagination and senses at their first meeting in York nearly two years ago? They had written regularly to each other since then and Dave, now at Oxford University, whilst she waited to go to the same place, had accumulated a rich sense of her wit, warmth and wicked sense of observation. And her love for Brighton.

He felt curious about and deprived of the sight of the person who had had such a liberating effect on his senses. There had been many interesting and enjoyable relationships with women that he had met on his European travels since York, but no one had been like Helen. He had rung on the spur of the moment and come down to see her.

Helen was deposited by a taxi on the station's cobbled approach, dressed in a tired fur top and faded jeans. Dave caught sight of her and the way her head loped to the right as she left the taxi made his heart race. How could she look so beautiful wearing such tatty clothes?

She gave him a hug, wrapping him in her fur arms, whilst suggesting that they take a coffee together further down Queens Road, before returning to her home. The confidence in her voice was surprising and encouraging, and it reassured Dave. He was full of the exploits of his European travels, and began to compare Brighton cafes with their Yugoslav or Turkish counterparts. Helen was amused and interested, whilst insisting on the unique ambience of Brighton.

They were both excited to find out how naturally they related, and one coffee led to another, and then a drink or two at the grand old Victorian pub on the corner of the side road leading to Churchill Square.

Helen regaled him with the exploits of the two Druids who lived in her home and stories of Brighton's underworld, of the control exercised and the terrible revenge delivered to individuals who betrayed a gang's code, including thousand tab acid trips off the pier. Her lurid sense of drama and the telling of her stories was as compelling in real life as it was in the flow of her regular letters to him.

They both shared a similar curiosity about the world and a delight in sharing or topping the other's story. So, when Dave reached out to take Helen's forearm, she responded by touching his hand. The attraction of the first meeting so long ago had continued undiminished, Dave realised triumphantly. He was relieved, as he knew the hollow disappointment of a second meeting after a first had seemed to promise so much. The intoxication of the rising warmth of this mutual sensuality, fed by alcohol, fuelled the next three hours. The other habitués had long since left the pub when Helen asked the bar staff, who had been watching them enthralled while washing the glasses, to ring for a cab.

They arrived at Helen's Edwardian semi-detached home at the back of Preston Park. Their mutual fascination quickly took them to her bed on the floor and a closer exploration of the physical attraction between them. They emerged, as the sun's strong rays brought in the glorious morning through the bedroom window, as one; overawed, imprisoned and liberated at the same time by what had happened.

Over the following weeks, the pretty bright red, purple and blue flowers in their neat beds in Preston Park bloomed. Their colours deepened into full maturity and then faded, exhausted by the heat. But the intensity of the sun and the power of Helen and Dave's feelings for each other continued undiminished.

And the sun shone. She shone, and she shone, and she shone ever more brightly, bathing the throngs of holidaymakers on the seafront, and sweeping the outlying hills cushioning Preston Park with a majestic, overarching blueness so that the seagulls seemed to crawk in unison with their happiness, basking in its warmth.

The abiding memory that Dave took back home was of Helen sitting beside the bedroom window watching the brilliant red sunset sprawl across the early evening sky after the long day's heat, a spectacular promise of a similar tomorrow. The intensity of their relationship, the hope for its continuance and the dark desperate cloud of fears if it failed, would last through many more summers.

The Red Dungarees
Hélène Meredith

Vanessa looked at the pile of clothes neatly folded on the table. A patch of red caught her eye and she picked it up. It was her son's little red dungarees. They held so many happy memories, she would be sorry to let them go to the charity shop. Her mother had bought them in one of those fancy French shops when bright colours were all the rage. Justin was three years old then. How could she forget! She could still picture him on the first day they met. It was a hot stifling summer and the foster family took her into the garden. There he was, cheeks flushed with excitement, running after a pet rabbit with ruby eyes. It had escaped behind a bush of crimson roses.

The following day the social worker allowed them to take him out for the afternoon. She carried him in her arms and they walked along a calm blue sea singing nursery rhymes together, his eyes the colour of the sky, looked at her wondering who she was but at the same time they were innocently trusting. They stopped at a cafe, by the lagoon. By the end of the meal, his turquoise anorak was covered with egg and tomato ketchup.

The following spring, he wore the dungarees again walking to the local park. He could not wait to get to the swings and started to run. A little bright spot moving in the green of the trees. He disappeared over the hill and Vanessa started to worry but she soon saw him sitting at the top of the slide in the middle of the lawn. It was another sunny day and a gentle yellow light played through the branches, warming the carpet of daffodils covering the grass. His blond hair had grown and he looked more self-assured. She bought him an ice cream and this time streaks of yellow covered the dungarees.

She was putting away the dungarees in a brown box when the phone rang in the hall. She wondered who it was at this time of the morning.

"Hi, Mum," said the voice. How strange she thought, the very person the dungarees belonged to: her son was now living in London with his partner.

"We have a surprise for you, Maria is pregnant."

How wonderful she thought. I'd better keep the red dungarees.

She had learned at painting classes that you could mix any primary colours together and get all the shades you wanted. Suddenly life was the colour of a rainbow. But for her, red was the colour of happiness.

Hooked On Crochet
Julie Gibbons

Auntie Doll loved to crochet. As a little boy in the 1950s I was fascinated watching her speeding fingers, crochet hook in and out. I suppose I wasn't your run of the mill boy. I enjoyed sitting and learning with her. I used to go to the village hall every week on a Thursday after school. Mum and Dad were both at work that day, so Auntie Doll had volunteered to sit with me. She didn't have any children herself, but she liked helping out.

"It's our craft afternoon anyway, so your Jack won't be any trouble. He's a good lad."

Although she wasn't really my auntie, in many ways she meant more to me than my family, for she really took an interest in me. The other ladies there babbled on about all sorts of things, their aches and pains, the time their husbands got home after a night at the pub, how much they'd spent at the butcher's. Most of the ladies called out to me when I arrived at the hall, but then they busied themselves with a good gossip. The hall seemed to stink of cabbage, for it was used during the morning to do cheap meals for the parishioners. Every week the ladies would squirt a bit of eau de cologne around to mask the smell.

Auntie invariably sat near the door. She always wore a brightly coloured scarf so I could see her as soon as I walked in the room.

"Now sit here, pet," she'd say patting the chair next to her. "Tell me about your best friend at school."

"He's called Fred."

"Yes," she encouraged, "Now what does he look like? Pretend you're a detective and you've got to describe him."

See what I mean? She made things exciting. After I'd described Fred, she asked about his character. I remember being puzzled by that.

She'd put down her work. "That might be a word you haven't heard. I'll explain."

So we sat for a couple of hours. She'd give me little exercises to do, and the crochet blanket, or whatever she was making, grew before my eyes. She was very clever. She could crochet, talk and listen all at the same time.

Auntie loved her food. She was almost as round as she was tall, although this didn't bother her in the least. She had an enormous bag at her feet, which contained all manner of exciting things, but always some tasty thing to eat. Chocolate digestives were our favourite, and we'd sit like conspirators chomping through the packet, regardless of the tuts from the other ladies.

"Jack I must tell you about our last trip."

Her Bert was never interested in travelling abroad, but they travelled extensively around the British Isles and she always sent me a postcard from her trips. Not the usual 'wish you were here' messages but interesting facts about where she visited such as the height of Blackpool Tower – five hundred and eighteen feet and nine inches, in case you wondered. She also told me the names of the different gates in York. All these facts were carefully explained. I've kept all the postcards in a box.

Auntie carried a small atlas in her bag. She used to show me the places they'd been on holiday. The visit to Cornwall filled me with stories of smugglers and caves. She spoke of pasties, a sort of meat pie, and of cream teas.

On the day she described this holiday she brought in homemade scones, which we smothered with jam and cream and ate, in secret, in the kitchen. Blissful times.

I kept shells from her holiday in Hastings on my window ledge, nudged against a little glass lighthouse she bought me from the Isle of Wight. It was really clever because it was filled with different coloured sands. She also brought back a stick of rock from Brighton which had writing going all the way through. When she went to London I received a telephone moneybox.

A book was always in her bag too, for she was an avid reader. Sometimes she would bring a dictionary and she would call out words and I would see if I could find them and read out the meaning. Auntie Doll was a friend and a teacher all in one. She taught me the capitals of different countries and helped me with maths, which I hated. I could tell her anything, things I wouldn't even tell my best friend. She never commented, just somehow made me see things in a different way.

As I got older, I no longer needed to be looked after on a Thursday. I could let myself in at home, make a sandwich, and get the fire started.

I still saw Auntie Doll around the neighbourhood. She was slower, of course, but still recognisable by the large bag over her shoulder. We always stopped for a chat. She told me they were closing the village hall on the Thursday, something about the increased cost of heating.

"Not to worry, Jack. Me rheumatics plays me up a lot these days, I like to stay in the warm. You take care of yourself," she said touching my arm. "You're a real credit to your Mum and Dad."

I can still remember feeling a lump in my throat when she said that. I watched her walk slowly along the road, a bright pink scarf round her neck.

Obviously, as I got older, I didn't see Auntie Doll so often. College, work and girlfriends became more important to me, but I would call in with a Christmas card and a bottle of sherry, and I never forgot her birthday.

After I graduated, I felt strongly about giving something back to the community. I decided to work with the elderly, which was the result, in no small measure, of my friendship with Auntie Doll.

It was several years later a neighbour told me she had died.

"Doll's niece is in the house at the moment. I know she'd like to see you."

It felt strange being in the house without seeing my old friend. "Auntie was very fond of you, Jack. Would you like something to remember her by?"

I remembered all the good times I'd enjoyed with the old lady, and what an influence she'd had on my life. I picked up one of the little crochet mats that I'd watched her make. I thought of the hours of loving work contained among the stitches. "I'll take this if I may."

I have treasured it ever since.

The Pond
Christine Maskell

There was a sparkle on the water. He had learned to swim in this pond when he was a boy, no more than five.

She thought back to that summer and could remember how the heat cast a shimmer on top of the water; how even the birdsong was muted, as though the birds were too exhausted by the continuous sunshine and stifling heat.

The poplar tree, with its feathery branches had offered some escape from the sun, its leaves weaving patterns across their arms and legs as they moved. They had brought a picnic but the water beckoned, sparkling in the sun as if to say "Come, play with me!"

They shed their shorts and tee shirts, leaving them in an abandoned pile and ran to the edge of the water. The shingle sloped gently here; it was possible to see the small pebbles clearly, and, if they stood very still, inquisitive tiny fish would venture around their ankles until some reflex movement startled them and they would dart away, the sand rising and clouding the water.

Further in the pond, the curve in the ground became steeper and the water deepened quite suddenly reaching her thighs, but the boy had shown no fear, his arms and legs had flailed like windmills and his mouth had been open in laughter as the cool water showered his face. He had disappeared under for a moment, re-appeared, spluttering and laughing, his uncoordinated actions raising a shower of bright droplets of water, which hung suspended in the sunlight, like a million rainbows, before falling back onto the pond's surface, to be replaced by more.

She had helped by holding his chin, keeping his head above water, avoiding the wildly splashing limbs, until the heat and the water had become too tempting, even for her. She had pushed the boy gently towards the shallow water and let go, submerging for a moment as she took two or three long strokes towards the middle of the pond. When she surfaced, she was 30 yards from the poplar tree. Her eyes searched for the boy.

She saw him. He was too far out to touch bottom, arms still waving frantically. Her heart stopped beating for an instance as she imagined him going under for the last time before she could reach him. But then he turned towards her. His wet hair was flattened to his head, his face turned up towards the sun and, with his eyes almost closed in joyous achievement, he said, "Look at me, Mum! I'm swimming." Then he disappeared once more under the water, only to pop up like a cork and splash and flail once more.

She breathed again, chiding herself for the moment of selfish pleasure and swam quickly to his side to guide him back to the shore. Later they laid in their wet underwear, under the semi-shade of the tree, drinking warm lemonade, feeling the droplets of water running down their bodies and the heat of the sun once more.

Even now, when the child was a man and she watched his children play, she thought she could still feel the heat of that afternoon.

A Raven Wept
Janis Thomson

I couldn't sleep. Constant itching on my back. Nothing my mother tried had helped. I got up to look out of the window. The lights from the South Bank skyline drew my eyes to Tower Bridge and the dark Tower of London nestling nearby. My GCSE history project that term was the chequered marital life of Henry the Eighth. I hated it at first. How could he have treated his wives so cruelly? Then, those few words my father spoke looking over my shoulder at what I was studying, changed hate to compulsion.

"Did I ever tell you we can trace a direct link to Anne Boleyn in our family tree?" he asked.

That changed everything! I became obsessed with the Tower of London and the Green where she was beheaded. I was there all the time. Every chance I had. All the Beefeaters knew me. They were very kind, and I became good friends with the gentle old man in charge of the Ravens. There were six of them. "Have to be six," he explained. "Any less and the legend says London will fall."

The itch was getting worse. I could feel two little bumps on my back. But that was the least of my problems! I wouldn't be able to visit the Tower much longer. We were moving. Away from London. My father had been so proud and excited when he came home from work earlier. He had been put in charge of his company's international business, and we were moving to Switzerland. I was devastated.

The feeling of being drawn to the Tower grew stronger than ever. So did the itch. Next morning, Saturday, I was at the gates at opening time and went straight to the Green. My friend the raven keeper was there, close to tears. "It's Mabel," he said. "She's dying." Mabel was the oldest of the birds. Lovely. Gentle. She used to sit on my shoulder gently stroking my back with her beak. If she could do that now it would surely ease this terrible itch.

That night was filled with dreams. Strange. Vivid. Huge black birds hopped on the balcony. Crowing. Staring at me with beady eyes. I counted. One, two, three, four, five. Mabel was dead.

My back ached now. I touched it. The lumps were bigger and I could feel stubble growing. No. Not stubble. Feathers! Unmistakable feathers! I looked down at my body. But it was not my body. It was the sleek black body of a raven, and the birds outside were beckoning eagerly.

Mayday in the Year of our Lord 1536

Did I wake, or was it still a dream? I don't know. But I was a raven now. Tentatively I stretched my wings and soared into the sky. I was exhilarated. This was meant to be.

But the River Thames was not the river I knew. No Tower Bridge. None of the buildings I was familiar with. Just green fields, and shabby houses lining the muddy banks. And boats. Hundreds of them ferrying passengers and cargo along the dirty, foul-smelling water. The noise was deafening. People shouting loudly. Carts and animals everywhere.

I swooped! I dipped! I dived! I performed!

And suddenly, forcibly, I found myself being drawn to the Tower of London.

The sun broke through as I passed the empty space that had been my home, and I flapped my wings in a last sad farewell to my parents. Then I was there. I was home! My five new companions acknowledged me as I landed next to them on a turret overlooking the Green.

I looked down. A beautiful woman emerged from the White Tower. She climbed the stairs to a platform and, with dignity, spoke to accept her fate and commend her soul to Jesus Christ.

The Green was packed with people. Many were sobbing. "God Bless you Queen Anne," they cried. A richly robed man was standing on the platform. Beside him was another dressed only in black. A cannon fired, and there was an eerie silence.

The man in black carried a long shiny sword behind his back. This was a public execution I was witnessing. The horror of it struck me. She was my ancestor, Anne Boleyn, and she was about to die the worst of deaths.

She was being handed a blindfold. She looked resigned to her fate, but before her handmaiden tied it, Anne Boleyn looked up at me with a sad and weary smile. I lifted my black, sleek head to the sky and offered the only goodbye I could.

A raven wept.

The Potato Peeler
Christine Maskell

Cold, dark winter Sundays,
Cosy kitchen, bright lights, oven warmth
Vegetables, a pleasing array
Spread out, awaiting attention.

Two forms, side by side, working
Peeling, chopping, cutting.
Little hands, inexpertly handling
The peeler, slowly, so slowly.
It's quicker alone

But no, this is special.

A memory, forever implanted
In a child's mind,
Retained long after I'm gone

Companionship and chatter,
All sentences a question
As slowly, the colourful array
Transfers from one pile to another

And the spread of peelings grows
Beneath this sturdy tool
How long before this everyday task
Becomes a chore for her?

How long before she finds an excuse
To be somewhere else?
Chooses other companions to me?
Sunday lunch will be late again
But does it matter?

Where Did that Come From…?

In and Out
Hélène says: I wrote this poem as a kind of therapy, shortly after I finished treatment for breast cancer.

Summer Loving
Julie says: the idea came from the song *Summer*

Loving in the film *Grease*. I chose her name because I imagined her parents were hippies.

Hove Beach
João says: this poem is bringing the movement of water, air, land, sky, people, to a canvas of words. I was looking at the sea, sound, light, forms, obviously from Hove sea front.

High and Endless Summer
Charlie says: this is taken from the first volume of *The Land of the Free Across the Pond 1971-75* and describes the second meeting of the central characters Dave and Helen.

The Red Dungarees
Hélène says: this story is partly autobiographical. Shortly after he was adopted, my mother bought some red dungarees for my little boy.

Hooked on Crochet
Julie says: one week Bridget bought in a collection of artefacts to the class and we had to choose an object to write about. My choice was a crochet mat.

The Pond
Christine says: we were asked to select a book, and take the first sentence from a particular page to write a story. I chose *Eden Close* by

Anita Shreve and it brought back vivid memories of teaching my daughter to swim.

A Raven Wept
Bridget says: this is one of many stories that grew out of a session on magic realism. (See also Janet the GP Receptionist). It all starts with the very ordinary character experiencing an itching sensation around the shoulder blades.

Jan says: This story came from an exercise we had in class when we were asked to write about suddenly sprouting wings. I think I was reading a novel about the Tudors at the time.

The Potato Peeler
Christine says: this is autobiographical, shared moments, first with my daughter, then later, my grand-daughter.

QUICK QUICK

This is how you do it: you sit down at the keyboard and you put one word after another until it's done. It's that easy, and that hard.
Neil Gaiman

Five Words

The Blue Man Woke Up and Said…

You Think Your Viewpoint is Original, do you?

Portslade Village Green

Where Did That Come From…?

Five Words

Ooops!
Pat Burt

Eric felt something tickling his moustache. A quick glance in the mirror revealed a large spider. Flaming Nora, he thought, and in his panic reached for the hammer to hit it.

Falling Flat
Liz Tyrrell

"It's a bit old hat, isn't it?"

His recently grown moustache made him look even more saturnine - thin and black it looked, as though it was only resting above his thin lips before taking off for somewhere else. She was irritated that someone so young had the power to say yea or nay. Panic began to set in.

"How do you mean "old hat"?" Protectively, she clasped the script to her chest.

"The Hammer House of Horrors was doing this kind of thing in the sixties."

She'd like to rip that moustache - probably an old prop he'd found somewhere - off his sneering mouth. Instead she tried to sound light hearted.

"Oh, it's not meant to be serious."

"That's just as well."

"I mean, a giant spider, it's just a spoof!"

He didn't look convinced.

"A lot of spoofs have been very successful lately."

Still doubtful. Oh well, she'd just go home and put a flame to it.

Christmas
Charlie Bowker

The children sat down for tea on Christmas Eve in front of the fluttering flames of the open winter fire. At the back of the hearth, a spider could be seen scurrying away from the warmth and the chatter of the little ones that were disturbing his peace and security.

They had just been read a winter horror story and were themselves feeling unsettled. It reminded Jimmy of the real life horror story unfolded on the news where a stepfather with a moustache set fire to his children's house because he was cross with their Mum.

Jimmy said he hoped Father Christmas wasn't like that when he came down the chimney. Mary told him off soundly. "You must be joking. Father Christmas is wonderful and looks just like our Dad!"

Nevertheless, the children had a difficult night dreaming about a jolly faced man with a white beard, who might or might not be their father or the madman with a flame thrower.

Never Quite Alone
Julie Gibbons

I was having a leisurely bath when there was an almighty hammering on the front door. It put me into a panic.

I got out of the bath in a rush, although I didn't forget to smooth down my moustache. Flinging on a robe, I made my way downstairs. I felt myself tense as I saw a familiar figure through the glass door. It was my old flame, Alicia. Lord, I thought I'd seen the last of her.

"John, John, hurry!" she said breathlessly, almost falling into the hallway.

"What now?" I was more than a little disgruntled thinking of the cooling bath.

"I'm so sorry, you must help me. There's this enormous spider in my room. I just don't know what to do."

Do they always come in threes?
Martine Clark

That poor spider's days were numbered now. It was running everywhere and I couldn't catch it. It was now right by the open fire, if only it would climb up the grate it would burn itself in the flame of the fire.

I started to panic, being terrified of spiders. I saw the hammer on the table and reached for it, trying to catch the horrendous thing and bash it, but it was always too fast for me. It hid right under the grate. I bent down and thought I've got you now.

A burning smell: I was too close to the fire. Oh no, I thought, I've singed my moustache and the spider's still alive and running into another corner. I was having a very bad day. What would be the third thing?

Spiders and Sheds
Michael Forrer

Lesley hesitated before approaching the shed. The building had been there when they moved in twenty-three years ago – and it was falling apart. He never liked going there. It was full of cobwebs. But he needed an old bucket to catch the drips from a leaking pipe in the airing cupboard.

He struggled to open the rusty catch and looked for the bucket. It must be right at the back behind the old petrol lawnmower we never use, he thought. A small movement caught his eye and he saw a small spider scurry from the bench, disturbed by the light. Instinctively he picked up the big old hammer lying next to the rusty saw and old nails. As Lesley turned to search for the bucket something much larger fell onto his hair from the ceiling. He could even feel the weight of the spider as it crawled over his brow and became entangled in his moustache. He shook his head in panic and the spider dropped to the bench. It was huge. Lesley swung the hammer, but missed the bench hitting the lawn mower petrol tank.

He did not see the spark. But he certainly felt the force of the explosion as the flame shot from the mower. He fell backwards through the doorway landing painfully on his backside.   For a few seconds Lesley watched as the flames spread.

No more spider. No more shed.

The Statue of the Blue Man Woke Up and Said…

Christine Maskell

"Why, when all around me is living and warm, am I trapped inside this shell? I cannot move away, I can only stand and watch life proceed without me being a part of it. People pass, they stop and stare before moving on. I am lifeless to them; they do not see that inside this shell beats a heart. Or that, one day, I will break free."

Martine Clark

"I can't open my eyes or feel my body but I feel so cold. That must have been some party. I can't believe my mates left me out here in this freezing weather. I think they must have stuck my eyelids down.

"Is there anyone there? Come on lads, joke's over. I can't bear this cold any longer, and for God's sake get me to hospital so they can use some of that stuff to release this glue from my eyes.

"Where are you? I'm getting scared now - please will you answer me. Please answer me! What is that? What's that sharp feeling, what's happening? Please no - not my legs, please don't hurt me. Who are you? No! Not my legs, don't cut them off. No! No!"

Liz Tyrrell

"Where am I?"

With difficulty he opened his eyes and looked around nervously. He soon discovered that the eyes were the only part of him that *could* move. When he tried to move his arms he found they were rigid in some ridiculous pose like a Roman senator or Greek god perhaps, one holding some sort of scroll, the other clutching his toga, some sort of flowing garment anyway.

His feet, too, were immobile, as though glued to some sort of high plinth that gave a commanding view of his fellow statues. At least he wasn't nearly naked like the bloke opposite with the strategically placed fig-leaf or the woman beside him with exposed breasts.

Charlie Bowker

The blue man woke up. It had been a long time, a very long time. He had lived thousands of years ago on the Greek island of Kos on the far side of the Mediterranean, the last stop before the old boat from Athens got to Rhodes. Kos was within sight of the Turkish mainland, not far from Bodrun.

There had been a vicious war, one of many over the centuries, between the two neighbouring countries in a dispute over who owned the islands. In this battle the Greek man, Antipideus, ran with his friends to hide in one of the caves down by the sea as the heavily armed Turks pillaged the old port of Kos town on the northern edge of the island. The invaders, brandishing scimitars and relishing the massacre of their enemies who had been caught off guard, spotted them and gave chase as they headed for the cave.

However, the terrified group of friends knew it was more than an opening in the rocks. The cave opened into a labyrinth, containing many interlinked and criss-crossing passages that the fabled Minotaur would have been proud of. Above their heads was steely, blue rock and above that, soft sand dunes. The blue man, or Antipideus the carpenter, as he was then, knew these caves well and that the Turks would never be able to find him and his friends. The invaders must have come to the same conclusion as they sealed the entrance before sailing triumphantly back across the short stretch of Mediterranean Sea to Bodrun.

Antipideus, realising that they were trapped, desperately scrabbled at the rocks now blocking their exit. They all tried, but the enemy had been thorough. They had no food and nothing to drink. Slowly and agonisingly they died of dehydration and starvation.

oOo

Gradually, over centuries, the bodies of the Greek men embalmed in the natural grave began to absorb the blue from the rocks. In 2012 a group of archaeologists intent on exploring Kos' fascinating mix of ancient Greek/ Turkish and Italian Renaissance heritage discovered the caves behind the well-weathered rocks by the sea.

They found all of Antipadeus' friends, blue and stone dead. The last figure was Antipideus, equally blue.

In deep confusion, he started to stutter….

You Think Your Viewpoint Is Original, Do You?

For Art's Sake
Liz Tyrrell

"You think your viewpoint is original, do you?" he says gloomily. "You sound like an old fogey." He goes into high-pitched Brighton. "I know what I like..."

"No, darling, it's just that..." She knows she'll have to tread carefully, Dan's his favourite son. "I only said that it's not what I'd call Art."

"And since when were you the expert?"

She studies the blank canvas that fills the wall in front of them. Well, blank to her mind, a vast expanse of beige splattered every now and again with random blobs of brown and orange. Her least favourite colours, she can't even say it's bright and cheerful.

Desperately she looks to the title for inspiration: *Study in Six Pieces*. What the hell is that supposed to mean? A price tag flutters from the frame. On the pretext of studying the painting more closely she walks over and peers at it. £6000? A grand for every piece? Bloody Nora! She knows her partner's son is hard up, but this is ridiculous.

Dan's father is on the attack now. "Just because it's not vases of flowers or country cottages it's not Art!" He's practically shouting, people are looking. "Do you know how long he was at college? Best in his year the tutors said."

This is not going well. One of the things they'd vowed in this relationship, a second chance for both of them, was to be honest with each other. And look where it's getting her.

She hates to do it, but tries the little woman approach. "Perhaps you could explain it to me then, darling. You're right, I am rather set in my ways when it comes to Art."

He stares into the void. "Well..." he begins. "Er..."

Compromise
Hélène Meredith

"You think your viewpoint is original, do you?" he said gloomily.

"No, I don't. You know I've wanted to do this for a long time. It's not as if it has come out of the blue. Try and look at it my way for a change. Instead of going through retirement without much to look forward to, we could take the plunge and start a new exciting life in France."

Here she goes again, he thought, she never gives up. It will be what she wants, not what I want. We've been arguing for nearly an hour and she won't give in. "It's all right for you, you don't have any problems with the language," he said.

"Neither do you. And anyway, you could take some classes once we are in the country, you'll be fluent in no time at all."

"You've not really thought this through properly, have you? It's not easy to sell a house these days, it might take months. Then, we'll have to find and buy another one. It'll take time before we get what we want."

"But think about what we could afford for our money, probably a large detached house with plenty of space and a decent size garden. Think of the long lazy summers, sitting outside sipping wine, eating French food on the patio. No more freezing winters, no more outrageous fuel bills."

"I don't fancy spending the rest of my life looking after a big house and a garden, it's just too much work. I want to be able to relax and enjoy my retirement. And what about the children? Once we are in France, we won't be seeing them very often".

"They can always come and visit and stay a few weeks in the summer. As it is, we don't see them very often, they have their own life to lead now.

"But if need be, it would be difficult for me to find a job in France to supplement our pensions. Everything has become expensive. And what if one of us becomes ill? We'll have to save money to pay for our treatment and take up some health insurance like the French do. We might not be able to afford it."

"No matter what I say, you'll disagree with me. The truth is, you don't really want to move, especially not abroad. It's too much of an upheaval and you are quite content with your life as it is."

"You may be right. So let's try to compromise. When I retire, we'll be able to spend more time in France. We could sell the house here and get a smaller place, like a bungalow or a flat. So we'll be able to pay the bills and travel. We'll keep our small holiday home in France, spend the winter months there in the warmth and come back to England for the summer months to see the kids. Then we'll have the best of both worlds."

"I suppose so," she says grudgingly.

Brothers' Meeting
Sallie A Sawicka

"You think your view point is original do you?" he says gloomily.

"No, not original," I say, "but sensible."

Edward heaves a sigh. "Go on, go on without me."

"I will then!" He begins to walk away up the beach.

"Wait," I call. "Don't go without saying goodbye."

Edward turns back again. "I don't want to say goodbye. I want you to come with me, Jono.

There's a place for you in the rocket. I don't want to leave you behind, my own brother."

"I won't be alone for long. There are thousands of us left in England, somewhere. I'll find them somehow."

"Look at it. There's nothing left here."

I look. There is an endless black pebbled beach with stark grey cliffs behind. A red-coloured sea and a mud-coloured sky. The sun is almost obscured by heavy smoke clouds. No trees or grass on the cliff top. All greenery perished by disease or fire.

I shiver. What a world.

"I'll make it out," I say. "I'll meet up with other people. Survivors. Better the devil you know..."

"How long do you think you've got? Come on, Jono, be realistic. How long before Lorcan collides with Earth? Two days? A week? As far as we can tell, it's on course."

"It may pass by! Scientists have been known to get things wrong," I laugh. Edward is a scientist.

"We weren't wrong about the sea levels rising. The unpredictable Gulf Stream. The earthquakes and tornadoes. The violent fire storms."

"I am not coming with you," I tell my brother. "I don't think your rocket will land on any planet, let alone take you to another galaxy. It's madness."

"Thousands have got away safely." Edward was always stubborn.

"Have you had any word back from any of them?"

"Our technology isn't up to it now."

"Exactly, that's my point. You will never get your miserable little rocket through the Van Allan Belt. The radiation will slice through the feeble sides of your craft. They knew the dangers two hundred years ago. They never really went to the Moon, now did they?"

"It's debatable I agree," says Edward, stiffly. "Now for the last time..."

"I'm staying," I say firmly. "Earth is my home. To go with you is to face certain death. To stay…Earth may be spared."

Edward looks at me. Irritation with his stupid younger brother and despair are written on his face. I can see all of that and more. "Then it really is goodbye?"

"Goodbye and good luck. You're all going to need good luck in that rocket of yours."

I watch Edward stumble up the beach and climb the cliff to where his air-car is parked. I watch as it takes off, its engine spluttering, reacting to the poor quality fuel. I sit down by the wine-coloured sea. As a gambler I know the odds are fifty-fifty. Will Lorcan hit the Earth or will it rush past into outer space? Who knows? All our computers are dead now and all our scientists are gone. But I am still alive and I wait for whatever may come.

Portslade Village Green

Mary Goldfinch

The sun is shining on the grass. Leaves are
covering trees in many shades of colour. Blue
sky above greenery seems to have white clouds.
Some, wispy, move slowly overhead.

Birds sing hidden in foliage. Cars make little
noise as they move along a nearby road.
People walk along some path near to where I
stand.

Over there, how wonderful, stands an old
park bench. It does not take much time to go
there, get a seat, which was made of fawn wood.

Liz Tyrrell

View from window
Bus toils uphill - jogger trotting
Mother puffs past with heavy shopping
The wind tosses foliage
A gaunt figure strides
Clamped to headphones
He doesn't see
Lush grassy space, a strutting black bird
Behind it all, pasted blue sky.

Pat Burt

Open space.
Cars, buses providing colour.
People strolling, some hurrying in summer
sunshine,
Hoping to avoid unscooped dog poo.
Birds playing in wind wafted tree branches.
Quiet oasis in fifty shades of green.

Where Did That Come From...?

Five Words
Bridget says: this is a creative writing exercise
that must be as old as written language. Pluck a
random word from a menu, a newspaper, a
novel and see where they take you. Sometimes
it's a dead end and sometimes it is the start of
something special. On this occasion the writers
had to include five words: panic, flame, hammer,
moustache, spider

The Statue of The Blue Man Woke Up and Said
Bridget says: I took a photograph of a statue at
Mill Cove House in 2010. It's a gallery on the

Beara Peninsula in Southwest Ireland where works of art live in the gardens.

You Think Your Viewpoint Is Original, Do You?
Bridget says: a line taken at random from a book can lead you anywhere.

Portslade Village Green
Bridget says: this was another quick exercise, intended as a limbering up before the class started properly. Students had to describe the village green that we could see from the room where we meet. Easy-peasy they thought, until I added that they couldn't repeat a word, *any* word including *it, the, and...*

This exercise is great for train journeys. Describe the carriage in between stations – the longer the distance the harder it gets. Why do it? Well, it forces you to rethink the way you usually structure sentences (although going down the poetry route solves some of the problems) and perhaps jolts you away from your customary vocabulary.

SLOW

A great lasting story is about everyone...The strange and foreign is not interesting--only the deeply personal and familiar. John Steinbeck

Lost and Found
Sallie A. Sawicka.

Please
Christine Maskell

It's A Sharp Tongue That Does Nobody Any Good
Sallie A. Sawicka.

Ted
Michael Forrer

The Vase
Martine Clark

At This Very Minute
Christine Maskell

What's Love Got To Do With It
Pat Burt

Icarus
Charlie Bowker

Homecoming
Liz Tyrrell

Food Glorious Food
Christine Maskell

Force Eight Gale
Sallie A. Sawicka

The Silk Dress
Liz Carboni

Lost and Found
Sallie A. Sawicka.

Sharon stood at the top end of the street market.
She looked along the length of the stalls. She
had only been a matter of minutes at Fred-the-
Fish buying their tea and in that time Margery
had gone. Vanished. The market was crowded.
It was difficult to spot her. Sharon walked out
into the middle of the road. People pushed past
her. She couldn't see her. Margery was lost.
Trying not to panic, she walked along the line of
stalls. A woman, standing in the middle of the
road, laden with shopping, surrounded by an
unruly brood of children, blocked Sharon's
progress for several frustrating minutes. She
darted sideways between the stalls and entered
the local supermarket. A quick tour of the shop
revealed no Margery.

Sharon headed for the street market again,
scanning the crowds. What was Margery
wearing? Not her old brown coat. No, she had
on her new cardigan. The cardigan was blue,
bright blue. Surely that colour should stand out in
the crowd? Then Sharon saw her. Half-way
down the market Margery was sitting on an
upturned wooden box chatting away to Vince-the
Veg.

Sharon began to run towards her, a
combination of anger and relief spurring her on.
She understood now why mothers smacked then
hugged their children when they saw them

running across a busy road, dodging the traffic by a miracle. She felt like smacking and hugging Margery right now. Sharon slowed down and walked up to Margery. Although she was breathless and shaking, she managed to appear calm.

"There you are," she said.

"Yes, here I am." Margery turned her head. "I've been having a chat with Vince."

"I've been looking for you."

"Have you? Well I said to Vince that I didn't know what those things are called. And he didn't believe me. He couldn't stop laughing, so I laughed too. What are they?"

"Oranges," said Sharon.

"They are very pretty. I don't think I've ever had one."

"Yes you have. You've eaten marmalade."

"If you say so," said Margery. It was clear that she wasn't at all sure.

"Come on. Vince has work to do." Vince had turned away and was dealing with a customer.

"Where are we going?" asked Margery, standing up.

"Home. I've bought fish for our tea."

"Are we going to your home or my home?" Margery looked uncertain.

"We are going to my home," said Sharon. "And after tea I'll take you back to your home."

"But have I got a home?"

"Oh, yes," Sharon said, and whispered to herself, "but I don't know for how long."

She took Margery's hand, intending to lead her back through the market.

"Oh, I do know you," cried Margery, "I didn't recognise your face. I'm not good with faces, but I know this hand. We've held hands before, haven't we?"

"Yes, Mum," said Sharon. "Yes, we have held hands before."

Please
Christine Maskell

Please can I have a man?
Perhaps on loan, just for a while.
A man who can do most anything
Around the house and make me smile
A man with adventure in his soul
To lift the tedium of the day
A strong arm for comfort
To pass the night time hours away
A man please, like Jack
A hero, they say, he won't come back
Taken by war, for the greater good,
Only a photo where the man once stood
I never thought him something special
Till now.

It's a Sharp Tongue That Does Nobody Any Good
Sallie A. Sawicka

Shall I compare you to a summer's day?
Dull and wet, with hair like rotting hay.
I laughed out loud when first you asked me out
I turned away, which left you in no doubt
I thought that you were reaching far too high.
As if a creep like you could touch the sky.
My friends exploded with delight at this.
They circled us, the scene too good to miss.
Your face, deep-pitted, turned a brilliant red.
Your blue eyes luminous with tears unshed.
Today, as I look back along the years
My eyes are clouded by unwanted tears.
To see you walk, your children by your side.
While I, unloved, regret my barren pride.

Ted
Michael Forrer

New job, new places, new responsibilities. It was
1975, not so long ago if you are old, but Neolithic
if you are young. I was twenty-four, visiting this
hospital - this former market town workhouse -
for the first time. The head nurse walked me
down to the wards. And I met those who had
been shut away, not because they were
dangerous or infectious, simply because they

had Down 's syndrome or had outlived the workhouse of their youth.

"Hello, Doris", said the charge nurse, as the elderly woman in an ill-fitting floral dress came up to look at me, the stranger. She came close, really close, and touched my face. "Come on, Doris", said the charge nurse.

It was on a later visit that I first saw Ted; sitting, sighing and smoking. To me he looked deep in thought, dreaming of other times and places. I learnt that this was Ted at his most expressive. Nursing Auxiliaries who had worked for twenty years in this grey old building could not recall him speaking; not a single word.

This place had been Ted's home for just over forty years. His round, brown, weathered face betrayed neither sadness nor happiness. I saw him often sitting outside on one of the old wooden chairs for a smoke before he resumed gardening, the one freedom this institution allowed him.

Usually he wore his battered brown hat and jacket, discarded by a park keeper long ago. Ted had no other belongings to call his own. The garden tools he used with care most days were not his. Others took his gardening clothes sometimes but he never argued. Many things were communal. The tea was made in one giant pot - milk and sugar included - and socks, pants and vests were kept in the one tall cupboard in the large, open, red-linoed ward dormitory.

Ted was mute, they said. Some perceived a quiet, patient dignity – and wanted to reach his intelligence, which, they supposed, might be deeply hidden. Anyone who spoke to him received the same response. Nothing. Except when he moved to obey staff instructions or to go out into the garden when permitted. Of course I tried to make contact, and always said, "Hello Ted" as I passed by, but there was never any reaction.

Many in the town outside this place labelled him and his fellow residents as mad. In 1975 "mentally handicapped" was the official label here – replacing past legal terms of lunatic or idiot – but soon to be rewritten as "learning disabled".

Changing labels did not change ignorance. They all signified different: not like me, put out of sight of those who don't have to care.

Months later we had progressed a little – individual underclothes and eventually a space each resident could call their own. And for a few the chance to live in a training flat, be taught, after decades in this regime, how to live life outside, escaping to their own home supporting each other with regular visits from a social worker. It was nothing short of a miracle. But not for Ted.

I talked to the charge nurse about Ted, and he pulled out his hospital records. They went back 20 years but were not very thick. The charge nurse had been there for decades too and knew Ted was always mute, but something made him find the previous volume. And together the two of us, like a couple of archaeologists, dug out the ancient history. We read of the 12--year old boy – who must have been so shocked and confused – arriving at this place. At that time there was no mention of mute. He still spoke – despite his fear. Over the weeks his hope must have dwindled, and the records showed that he spoke less and less and after some time, not at all. That was that. Staff changed and they, and perhaps Ted himself, forgot. Infrequent entries in following years would record the occasional illness or routine examination – and just add the word "mute".

Had they read the ancient records, the doctors passing through would have known that this country boy went to the workhouse as an alternative to prison. His crime – stealing two stamps at the local post office. Was he guilty? Who knows? His family visited initially and then embarrassment, hardship or neglect meant that contact was lost.

Ted's silent message was one of betrayal by all whom he loved, of a trauma so devastating that his defence was to build walls around his heart even stronger than the stone walls of the workhouse. The workhouse became a hospital; the National Health Service took over in 1948 with slightly better food and a regime not quite as harsh. But still new staff arrived believing there was a good reason for each inmate to be there: mad, bad, or not.

In the later seventies a handful of heroic residents were taught independence – to cook and shop and help each other. Doris was one of them. Some years later I went back to the town and someone tapped me on the shoulder. I turned and saw Doris who invited us back to her home where we had tea.

But no miracle for Ted. He had found long ago that retreat was his only way forward and survived in the company of his friend – the garden.

The Vase
Martine Clarke

A love so strong,
So smooth, so right,
At first without a crack in sight.
One little chip
No one would know,
Turn it round
So it won't show.
Another crack
That's not so bad,
Even though it makes me sad
To watch the beauty slowly break,
Another crack's so hard to take.
Until it topples hard and fast,
This vase wasn't meant to last.
Now in pieces, it's fallen apart,
Now I have a broken heart.

At This Very Minute
Christine Maskell

The silence reverberated through the large
house. Upstairs, Gloria was completing her
make up. She had discarded several outfits,
which were on the floor waiting for her maid to
hang up. Today, she was certain, the call,
offering her a part, would come. She had
contacted her agent, asked him to spread the
word that she had been offered a big part in a
new blockbuster. Of course she hadn't, but it
was guaranteed to stir interest. Once her name
came up, they would all be after her again. She
stood up and preened in front of her full length
mirror, imagined she was in front of the camera
and posed, her head held coquettishly to one
side and liked what she saw. Slim, with good
legs, her long hair glossy, skin glowing and not a
line to be seen, what's not to like, she thought.

I'm easily as beautiful as Elizabeth Taylor, in
her younger days of course; but Meryl Streep is
always first choice. Not that I would have
accepted *The Iron Lady* part, who would want to
appear old in a film? No, I need a role that
shows off my beauty.

She took another self-satisfied look in the
mirror. Her brows were plucked carefully; the
eye shadow enhanced the blue of her eyes; the
crow's feet had been removed and her skin
stretched wrinkle free. The gloss accentuated
her full lips, the whole effect had cost more than

$50,000 but had been well worth it; she looked thirty again.

She rather wished she had a Burton, someone she could "be seen with", who would adore her, buy her jewellery, and tell her she was beautiful. Where had they all gone? Some had been pleasure seekers like her; others were dreadfully dull and had wanted commitment and marriage. Marriage! As if she would have risked getting pregnant, having stretch marks and sagging breasts. Too late now, and if truth be told, she couldn't really remember all their names.

She peered closely at the mirror; it wouldn't do to have the grey showing through. She made a mental note to book the hairdresser for tomorrow. She checked her watch and checked her phone again; surely the call would come soon. Perhaps she should drive into town, be seen in Mario's, but not alone, that would never do. Perhaps with her agent, although the last few times she had suggested it, he had been too busy. Well, he's not much use anyway, maybe I should try another. In any case there were usually one or two starlets at Mario's hoping to be photographed with someone famous. The last thing she wanted was for them to be photographed with her!

She went downstairs, poured herself another large whisky, put her sunglasses and sun hat on and sat in the shade, carefully posed and gazing across the pool towards the driveway. She could hear the phone from here. Why, at this very minute, there was probably some casting director looking up her number.

What's Love Got To Do With It
Pat Burt

Parlez moi d'amour,
Speak to me of love. I would settle for speak.
Where did our love go? Another song.
Ours is playing hide and seek.
The dog gets more attention, the cat gets all the strokes.
Perhaps I should stop de-fuzzing, grow furry like the pets.
Sit up and beg, jump on your lap, weave in and out your legs.
Where did our love go? It's playing hide and seek.

Icarus in Wandsworth
Charlie Bowker

Oxford 1973
Ambition lit his flame

He told us all his name
So we could chart his fame
But Paul-fruitgum was, for him, our name

London 1983
Reuters gave him one of six
But Chris aimed much, much higher at a
National Ball
Star Guardian Indie journalist
But this was not enough. He had to have it all

London 1993
He knew the future before it came
The end of left Labour, rise of SDP, Lib Dem
was all the same
If Chris was leader and the party was hewn
Around his name. This really was his game

Brussels 2003
And now he was the rising ecological star
Dominant MEP, Kyoto and then the speeding car
From Brussels where he jumped with ease
Nearly to lead his party, twice, to glory and the
highest seas.

Wandsworth 2013
But hell hath no fury like a woman scorned;
The lies, the lies he told, and all the law
suborned
From Coalition Cabinet minister to the gates of
jail,
The pride, the sin of hubris has such a sting
within its tail.

Homecoming
Liz Tyrrell

I pull the warped rock of sliced bread out of the freezer - heaven knows how long it's been there - and give thanks. Strange how something so mundane makes me so happy.

I peer into the damp bag, not daring to read the sell-by date. The white slices cling together. I can't even wait for them to defrost, but insert a sharp knife between the thin slabs and wiggle them free.

The toaster has been idle for so long it exudes an unappetising smell of hot dust and stale breadcrumbs. No matter. I shove in two brittle segments, slump down and wait. I'm home.

While it cooks I throw my coat onto a chair, heave my case into the bedroom and scoop up the mountain of post heaped beneath the letter box.

Even as I scan the mail I think of toasting crumpets with Gran, who squatted in front of the range, face reddening as she thrust the brass toasting fork towards the coals, snatching at the crumpet when the other side needed doing. After her knees gave out we bought her a Russell Hobbs four-slice.

I hear her voice. "What do you want to go and live in that God forsaken country for?" A week in the Isle of Wight was abroad enough for her.

"You won't be happy!" Now she can say "I told you so!"

At Gatwick I bought milk and butter - a lovely salty brick, not that insipid continental stuff. The toast pings up smartly. Even as I scrape the butter across the patchy brown surface, two more slices, cold and spongy now, are in the toaster. The thawed bread in the bag feels much softer, it crumbles to the touch. The soggy bag gives off a slightly woody smell.

The butter pools onto the chewy toast, I suck it off, relishing the salty creaminess. Reluctantly I investigate the post. A soft airmail package with the dreaded handwriting. The scarf I gave him for Christmas. I leave greasy fingerprints all over it and push it under the chair.

The next two slices announce their arrival. People "over there" might sneer at the much derided English "blotting paper" or "cotton wool", but they can keep their brown bread, their grey bread - for heaven's sake - and, especially, their black bread. My teeth sink comfortingly into the last slice.

Food, Glorious Food
Christine Maskell

The party had been really good, everyone had enjoyed themselves and the food had gone down well, with lots of compliments to his Mum. She was such a good cook, John thought. He loved it when there was a family celebration. His sister and brother had both married and produced offspring, so there had been no pressure on him to do the same. Just as well, he was happy living at home with Mum, she was a great cook, and she washed and ironed his clothes just as she used to do when he was growing up.

As usual, he had made sure he had eaten the lion's share of everything during the evening and was feeling comfortably full. The clearing up was the part he liked best really, it was always the rule that Mum cooked and he disposed. She almost always prepared far too much, but, she said that he was a big man, needed feeding well and, in any case, supposing someone calls just as we're sitting down to eat? "Best to be prepared." John never argued with that.

What she didn't realise was that, instead of throwing the leftovers away when he cleared up, he ate everything. Well, it was all so delicious, it would be almost criminal to throw it away. It wasn't as if he was really full or anything. Tonight, of course, she had cooked for twenty. For a while he thought everything was going to be eaten and he had fretted about how he could secrete some away for his supper, but it had been okay.

Now, after everyone had left and Mum had gone upstairs to bed, he sat at the kitchen table and began to eat. First the sausage rolls, flakes of the pastry falling on his sweater as he bit into the still succulent centre. Next, the two slices of pizza, not so good cold, but too good to throw away. He spread pâté thickly onto the few pieces of bread remaining. Potato salad was one of his favourites and he got a large serving spoon out to eat that, chewing hurriedly and pushing more into his mouth as he swallowed. The lettuce leaves he discarded, he only liked salad covered in mayonnaise.

His other favourite was the chicken drumsticks and he had put some to one side earlier, just for this moment. He bit into the soft flesh and, hot or cold these were so good he could eat them all day! He chewed on the bone, sucking to make sure every piece of meat had been eaten before reluctantly discarding it and picking up another.

Everything looked and tasted wonderful, particularly when there was no-one else around and it was all his. Even so, the urge to grab as much as he could and cram it into his mouth was strong, in spite of being alone. He reached for a third drumstick, chewed quickly and swallowed, trying hard to put as much in his mouth as he could whilst reaching for another.

He spluttered and coughed as a large mouthful lodged in his throat. Something sharp dug in and he couldn't move it. He banged his chest, trying to dislodge the food without success. He struggled to breathe, his face turned red, his mouth opening and closing as he gasped for air. He couldn't believe this was happening; he hadn't finished eating everything yet!

He tried swallowing again, biting into another dense piece of chicken but now the need to breathe was greater than the need to eat and he looked around desperately for help. He felt peculiar, unsteady, and little pinpoints of light were flashing in front of him as he swayed. He reached for another drumstick, and fell heavily to the floor, clutching at the tablecloth. He laid there, with the remains of the party food around him, still clutching the drumstick, chest heaving for a moment, until with a shudder, his eyes closed and he lay still.

Force Eight Gale
Sallie A. Sawicka

Force eight gale in the channel, squally showers,
Heavy rain.
No one lingers in the streets,
We nip smartly from our heated rooms
To our over-heated rooms
To our over-heated cars.
I gave my overcoat to Oxfam.
Unused for five years
The world's green–house problems began in my car.

Weather happens to other countries,
Not to us.
Potato fields flooded? Fly from Israel.

A blight on the wheat crop?
Serve extra rice.

Tesco is our shield
And Sainsbury's our salvation.

Force eight gales in the channel?
Shut the curtains,
And pull up the drawbridge.
Hastings hit by a hurricane?
Trawlers missing in the channel.
"Yes, I saw it last night on the telly.
Do you know I can't buy any fresh fish today?"

The Silk Dress
Liz Carboni

Chapter One

Mortal mouths, fragile mouths, so small but alive,
all those prayers had been used and these bony
little angels without wings at last were birthed.
    Marie Therese had been fighting for her life for
hours in the cold sea; her labour pains had been
overruled only by her desperate desire to live.
    Bedouin women gathered on the beach. The
storm showed signs of spitting out some bounty,
but the ship had taken no time to slip beneath
the waves, they would find nothing of value
today. Battered pieces of wood drifted towards

the shore and the women waded out to drag them onto the beach. Half submerged in the weeds of the shallow water, they found Marie Therese. They could see she was young and dying. Her dark matted hair masked her contorted face. Between them they supported her struggling body and laid her on the warm sand, holding her while she gasped for breath. The dark green sea had penetrated her lungs and her spasms and moans were surely her death throes. Her clothes were torn but still of a piece, the fine silk of her long dress had billowed and kept her afloat.

Over the dunes the men of the tribe appeared on camels, and from their loftier view, they had seen the activity on the shore. They just caught sight of the ship breaking up on the rocks and saw it sink fast. It would be days before anything of value would spill out onto the sand. The possibility of gain made them decide to delay their onward journey for a few more days, to see if the ocean would bless them.

The writhing of the sodden woman suddenly produced another reaction from the swarthy few, as tiny cries mixed with the wind. A baby, bloody and small, was emerging from the now deflated green gown. Its mother motionless in the sand, but like the child, she was actually breathing.

The Arabic chatter filled her ears; she was used to this noise but could glean no information from it. She knew her body had expelled its load but had no strength to heave her still heavy torso to gather it up.

"Please don't move me," she tried to speak but no sound left her lips. The sand cupped her like the feather bed she had been sailing towards. Had she reached her childhood home after all? Yes, yes and she could hear her grandmother giving orders to move her to a warmer room. The cold of her empting body made her shudder uncontrollably.

She looked towards the late day sun pleading with it to warm her. She, the sun and the sand were all slipping away

The sun and moon exchanged places several times before she started to return to her body, she felt her breasts being nibbled by the fish; so she hadn't made the shore after all. More sunsets passed but the little fluttering fish persisted.

Jean Claude Alexandre was looking out to sea from the roof of his house; from here he had a clear view of the port and of his ships being loaded and unloaded. Sending Marie Therese to France was the right thing to do, he was sure of that; Casablanca was no place to give birth. He should have had word by now. The short trip to Tangiers and then the crossing on to Marseilles would take only three or four days. Still no message had come.

She had only been gone for such a short time, but already the house was suffering. The smell of her, the sound of her feet paddling along the tiled floors, her long graceful limbs emerging from her silken robes and her skin blushed amber by the high sun. He could hear her singing and see her brushing her dark, shiny, date coloured hair. He ached for the very sight and sound of her. He looked to the dark sky, it matched his mood. Perhaps he had panicked, when the old Fatima kept tutting and rolling her eyes every time she looked at Marie Therese. He remembered that look from three years ago when his first wife was at the same stage of her pregnancy. He had not heeded her then.

Marie Therese's life could not be risked; he sent her on his ship back to France. She was in the safe hands of his captain and friend Michel Gautier. The short journey on to her grandparents farm would not take too much of her strength, she was strong. He would follow after the lambing, in time for the birth.

His Moroccan sky was unusually dark that day and shadows fell quickly on unusual places; doom seemed to be spelling out words he was unable to read.

Building this house had proved difficult; he was determined to have his house on the piece of land he had chosen years before. The plot was well outside the city wall and in an area still prone to Barbary bandit attacks. Europeans and Moroccans alike all told him he was mad to build there. Because he brought men from Spain and Portugal to construct the huge garden walls, the local workers were slow to warm to him. It took much haggling from local craftsmen to gain contracts and beautify the floors and gardens with the vibrant tiles he had come to love. The presence of a Moroccan workforce together with the high walls seemed to deter the bandits, and the attacks trailed off. Eventually Jean Claude and his house were accepted with pride and seen as source of work and income. When he brought his lovely new wife home she seemed to enhance his status and charmed everyone who came to their door.

Just as he hoped, Marie Therese inhaled Morocco; like him, she loved its sounds, revelled in its colours and felt part of its rich earth. Most of the time, in keeping with her position as wife of a wealthy French ship-owning merchant, she dressed in the silks he imported, served food and wine sent from his estate in Lyon and sat at tables made by Parisian artisans. But when left to her own devices, she wore robes and jewellery she found in the souk, tied her hair in the same way as the Fatimas and allowed her skin to breath in the sunlight. She delighted in feeding the animals and working in the garden. She was so unlike the previous Madame Alexandre, with her ease and natural empathy that she fascinated most people who came in contact with her. Travelling Bedouins, masons looking for work, wives of his countrymen all terrified of leaving the Medina, they all came; they couldn't keep away.

Jean Claude Alexandre was a pioneer like his father; he was brave, mad and bad of course, and a giant of a man with great dreams and plans. Most of his plans centred on Morocco, a place he loved and cleaved to. As a small child his father had taken him there from the family's summer house in Gibraltar. He took gold time-pieces and silks to trade with the Sultans and Sufi leaders.

Trade was uppermost in his father's life and he took his son on epic journeys along the coast, and deeper into Africa. To colonize and make Mother France rich was fixed in his heart and to bring home all things fantastic to his French lands confirmed his achievements. Perhaps in the wake of the British acquisitions in India, the French and Italians were prompted to mimic their efforts a little closer to home. The Italian cousins were more focussed on Tunisia and Libya while the French concentrated more on Morocco and Algeria. In this late part of the nineteenth century treaties and exchanges abounded. The politics of it all had begun to frustrate his father and he looked about for new adventures.

New promises called from Madagascar, riches of spices, plants, and trees which could flourish in France and Morocco; they bore the fruit and flowers that would grace his lands for ever. He left with orders big enough to fill his coffers for years. They had no news of him, he never returned.

Although Jean Claude entered manhood fatherless, he carried all his father's strength and ambitions and with his fierce and controlling mother, he was able to embark on the journey prepared for him.

When it was time to marry, his mother found Louise. She had arranged her, presented her on a family silver salver and cocooned her in embroidered linen displaying the intertwined crests of their prestigious backgrounds. She was shy, small and her blue eyes were tinged with sadness. She was the youngest and only surviving child from her own litter. Her brother Xavier Paul had perished in Senegal with a fever at the turn of the century, and her brother Philippe died a few years later in the Mekong River with the colonialists. They were attempting to link the river to the Indochinese colonies, both were unmarried.

Their father had been felled in the first Franco-Dahomean war in the early 1880's when Louise was a baby. He had travelled to West Africa in the firm belief that to colonize great swathes of Africa would be of great advantage to his beloved France. Both she and Jean Claude had been made fatherless by covetous ambition.

Louise's withered mother had pushed her into marriage with the wealthy Alexandres. Two sons in two years was the only requirement; so she set about fulfilling the dreams of her mother and her new mother in law. Pregnant within weeks of the contract and enthroned within the confines of her husband's Moroccan domain, she was performing her role of a brood mare perfectly. Jean Claude was always full of excitement about the lands he had claimed outside the city walls of Casablanca. He delighted in showing her his plans for the new house his Spanish workers were constructing for them and their sons.

The night she went into labour he was out drinking with a German acquaintance, Max. He and his pretty wife had recently moved into the medina, they lived near him in a villa owned by the railway company. Germany needed a foothold in North Africa, and a few ruthless men like Max had been sent to achieve it. That night Jean Claude quickly tired of all the politics Max's friends' spouted and objected to his old drinking haunt being taken over by their loud and conspiratorial behaviour. Casa Blanca was changing; he knew it was.

When he left the bar Jean Claude was met by two worried servants who had been looking for him for some time, they spoke in hushed tones. Louise was not due for another four weeks, but he sensed disaster. Arriving at the house he found uproar, both Fatimas were sobbing in true Arabic fashion with that high pitched gurgle interrupted by choking and coughing, much hand wringing and pacing was taking place.

A filthy robed hag was wrestling with poor Louise who seemed demented with pain; sweat and blood were pouring from her swollen body. "Where is the Doctor, dear Lord what is happening here?" Jean Claude was screaming at all the onlookers, but not one pair of eyes met his. His anger and fear sobered him and guilt and deep despair engulfed him. Just before dawn a weak cry from Louise heralded the birth of a scrawny girl child. He cradled the mother and child to his chest. He had never noticed before how small Louise was, naked and white she reminded him of a shorn goat. Louise died in his arms.

Marie Louise Alexandre was the image of her dead mother and her father lamented her gender and her weakness. If she was going to survive he had to send her to the grandmothers in France.

In this first decade of the twentieth century enormous changes were taking place all over Europe with an emphasis based on North Africa. Treaties were drawn up and long held arrangements were being questioned and refuted. In the French government, men in high places, with connections to Morocco, were hastily being removed from office. Many of the old potentates gone and a puppet Sultan ruling from Tangiers to the edge of the Spanish Sahara. Morocco was changing. Jean Claude could see it was all for the taking, dynasties could be established, fortunes made, it was sons he needed. Letters came from the two Grandmothers, the child was well enough, but prone to all the ailments. "When would he come to see her?" "Soon," he replied.

Guilt for the death of his wife and his lack of feelings for his daughter were hard to admit. In time he moved into his grand empty house, the Fatimas swept and cleaned but still cooked in the courtyard. His horses and their grooms slept in splendorous stables but he slept in a lonely bed in a room fit for a monk.

Jean Claude's drinking and violent tempers were destroying his business and even his devoted workers at the port tried to avoid him. At home the servants took the brunt of his anger and the few friends he had left, were concerned about him.

Max sent his pretty wife Elise with an invitation for him to attend a dinner party. On the morning she arrived he was in yesterday's clothes, unwashed and stinking of last night's brandy. How French she was! Holding a handkerchief to her nose she toured the room pretending not to see his disarray. He made no attempt to excuse his state, but sat, still in his boots, open legged, holding his chin, viewing her as he would view a new horse. Would she be bidden, could she be ridden? She was married to a bore of a man, it wouldn't be difficult, no complications, no recriminations, he really needed the comfort her soft pale skin. By the end of her visit and with a single kiss of farewell, they both knew how it would be.

The Villa Alexandre stood defiantly outside the city walls, its own walls still harsh and white waiting to be dressed in flowers and vines. For more than two years Jean Claude had promised himself he would spend time in France buying furniture and visiting his family, his little daughter was waiting. At last he left for France, he would return with all the trimmings that would furnish his house and sheep to better his herd.

Unlike her predecessor Marie Therese was not presented to him; he found her, won her and loved her. She did not come wrapped in wealth; she had been orphaned early and reared by her maternal grandparents on their farm near Marseilles. Jean Claude was stocking his new lands with the wonderful horned sheep they bred and found himself returning over and over again to arrange and re-arrange their deliveries to his ships. It took less than six months for him to make her his bride and deliver her too to the huge tiled house outside the city walls of Casa Blanca.

Material swaddled Marie Therese's upper body; she rubbed her face against her shoulders and felt its softness. Her eyes were struggling to open but at last she was emerging from the turmoil of her dream world, and yet the little fishes were still nibbling. She made to move her arms but both hands were bound fast holding little warm orbs to her breasts. Sucking noises emitted from them and her breasts were pulsing. Babies. Two babies. Her babies, yes. So she had birthed two little souls.

Shifting her hips and pushing her heels down into the carpets that supported her, she lifted herself into a sitting position and gazed down at her own fecundity.

Through her misty mind, sounds and images floated back to her, the ship, oh God, the ship. She shot her head up expecting to see the mast and the sea high above her, but above her now was a smaller mast and huge bright red blankets enveloping her with quiet and warmth. The Bedouin tent felt familiar and the low hum of

Berber Arabo was beginning to make more sense. Faces and whispers were emerging from the dark edges, light brown limbs clothed in pale silk shifts and pantaloons and with hair wrapped loosely in the soft fabric she felt against her skin, all came closer and touched her.

From his viewing perch Jean Claude saw his men coming and dreaded to hear what news they bore. These men never left his warehouses on the natural harbour where his ships docked. In faltering French mixed with Arabic they told him.

The wailing that reared up from within the house reminded him of that other loss and a tumour of grief started to grow in his heart. That high pitched Arab sob punctuated by choking and coughing was seeping from him too.

Slowly he understood the details of the earthquake, barely felt on land but which had erupted under the sea shortly after his ship had set sail.

He knew these old men held an undying belief in the power of natural forces, tempests, torrential storms, fires and quakes and that they held firm to the animistic lore. This rumbling sea had a soul and could bring forth both life and death, they urged him to hope. *Um sh Allah.*

Ships slowly started to return to the harbour all with tales of loss and destruction. Jean Claude begged them all for signs of where his ship might have washed up, and they looked to the sky and made hand movements that told him nothing. He went with his ships to search for her, his captains would not listen to his pleas to go further south. Weeks passed and Jean Claude faded and folded into his pain, the Fatimas' wailing reduced to a low tearful moan. No one called at the house and even her garden retreated back into the soil.

The tribe had delayed their departure for many days but had benefited from the bounty eventually spewed up from the ship that had landed Marie Therese. Urgency now whipped through the camp. It was time to resume their caravan; the men were making ready the pack mules and feeding the camels the wet food that would enable them to sail into the desert. The women lingered over the babies, still amazed they had saved them and their mother. She was strong now and possessed a much admired physical strength and courage, they would live.

Marie Therese had nothing to pack and saw that a donkey had been tied up to the flotsam as her mount. That evening a huge sheep was killed and roasted on the central fire and the whole tribe sat together and devoured the sweet smelling mechoui. Then, in celebration, they danced, the men with the men and the women with the women.

She swayed to the music coming from the drums horns and pipes and wished Jean Claude could know she was safe. The women, assuring her that she too had to eat and drink in readiness for the journey, pressed more food and an unfamiliar thick juice on her. She sank into sleep ready for the journey north.

The familiar mewing of the babies woke her; they were cradled together in a carpet lined nest just out of reach. Her movements were slow and fuddled; the lapping of the waves sounded louder than usual and a strange silence surrounded her. Oh no, no, no, they were gone, they had left her. She was alone, but for her babies and a lactating donkey.

Oh dear God…

Where Did That Come from…?

Lost and Found

Sallie says: an inspirational teacher of English was struck down by Alzheimer's disease. In an article about the effects of this illness, her husband wrote of her response to small familiar things. The sound of his voice. A much loved piece of music. The touch of his hand. Sadly, at the end even these small miracles failed.

Please

Bridget says: we read and discussed Selima Hill's poem *'Please Can I Have a Man'* in class and for homework I suggested writing a wish-fulfilment poem.

Christine says: we had been discussing poetry in class and homework was to attempt a sonnet, imposing a contrast from line nine.

It's a Sharp Tongue That Does Nobody Any Good
Sallie says: in this sonnet I celebrate the triumph of the bullied over the bullies. It does happen, although it sometimes takes almost a lifetime to overcome.

Ted
Michael says: workhouses were closed before World War Two, officially, and some of those buildings became NHS hospitals in 1948. But nearly thirty years later I discovered that some workhouse residents were still living there. Ted was one of those forgotten.

The Vase
Martine says: the idea for the vase came from writing a metaphor about love and seeing a much loved old vase with a crack running through it.....

At This Very Minute
Christine says: This developed from a classroom exercise where we were each given a photograph and asked to develop a character from it.

What's Love Got To Do With It
Pat says: I don't 'do' poetry - so where this came from - who knows!

Icarus In Wandsworth
Charlie says: Chris Paul-Huhne was an Oxford colleague I knew slightly. He was editor of *Isis* and gained a first in PPE before a very successful career (minus the Paul!) in journalism and politics, rising to be a Cabinet minister in the Coalition government. Unfortunately, it all went spectacularly wrong in over the break-up of his marriage and the illegal transfer of penalty points to avoid a driving disqualification. Chris has always had a good sense of humour so I hope he will forgive me this opportunity to write a light hearted mock Popean piece of doggerel, catching his very real ambition and, probably temporary, very public demise. In class we were asked to write a poem based on the classic structures.

Homecoming
Liz T says: this grew out of an exercise in class that came soon after a trip to Germany when we were given the – to my mind – unpalatable black bread on the homeward flight. This bread and its foreign connotations seemed to find its way naturally into this passage of writing.

Food, Glorious Food

Christine says: this was inspired by a short story competition entitled 'Seven Deadly Sins'.

Force Eight Gale

Sallie says: I tried to show how real life is often removed from people's reality.

The Silk Dress

Liz C says: one week Bridget told us to go to page 101 of any novel we had at home. We had to use the first complete sentence that didn't include a character's name or a place as the first line of our story. I actually used page 99 of Joseph O'Connor's *The Star of the Sea* because I'm a bit of a rebel like that and there I found an extraordinary sentence about bony little angels without wings. I'm not sure why but it awoke memories of a long forgotten family legend about a pregnant woman shipwrecked on the shores of Morocco. Very little else is known so I'm free to invent. To my surprise I find I am writing my first novel.

DANCING THE OLD FASHIONED WAY

Life can only be understood backwards; but it must be lived forwards. **Søren Kierkegaard**

Dancing Through My Youth
Maggie Wright

My Very Special Dad
Sally Wood

If It's Not Broke
Janis Thomson

How To Jog Your Memory
Hélène Meredith

I Remember
Mary Goldfinch

The Sleeping Beauty Town
Hélène Meredith

Birthday
Maggie Wright

The Unopened Letter
Janis Thomson

Sundays
Hélène Meredith

Dancing Through My Youth
Maggie Wright

In all humility, for someone who loves to dance, I have not done nearly enough. But there is a dance I have revisited hundreds of times in my memory.

I was one of nine children living in a rural village in Ireland. It was the late fifties and I was around six or seven. Like millions of children all over the world our mother told us stories of how she met our father. That would have been in the forties, the age of Hollywood and the 'Big Bands'.

When she began to recall these stories we flocked to her like magnetic cut-outs around her chair. In her young days there were no cars, so groups of boys and girls had to make their own way to the dances.

She painted pictures of them tramping the roads lit by moonlight. If you were lucky you might get a lift on the crossbar of a bike and the occasional flash lamp was always to hand if pitch dark. I imagined the noisy chatter of young people filling the winding lanes in the black of night; all of them in search of fun. I felt the excitement of the anticipated dance and the first thrill of something forbidden.

She and Daddy met at one of those dances and he won her heart by being the best dancer of all.

As my sisters and I grew up, our house was full of laughter and music. The neighbours loved to tell us how everyone watched when Mammy and Daddy took to the floor.

Many years later when a lovely waltz came on the wireless - one favourite was *The Tennessee Waltz* - and we caught her on a carefree day, she would stand up and we children watched in bewilderment as she changed from our work weary mother into a tall shapely woman. Head held high and shoulders back, her face was set in remembrance of long ago.

It was a solemn occasion as round the kitchen she swept us each in turn, to cries of, "Can I be next, please?" She did not do this lightly and sometimes she would stop abruptly and say, "That's enough now, I have work to do" We never argued, her *voice* told us it had stopped and those who had not had a turn were bitterly disappointed.

Thinking back, it must have cost her to conjure up the carefree girl she was before the work and worry of a large family. We were not a 'huggy kissy' family, but those brief seconds of being held in our mother's arms were breathtakingly lovely. Time and all its worries just stood still.

In our teens - it was now the early sixties - the traditional way to spend Sunday afternoon was to walk down from the village to the river which was the dividing line between north and south. It was very picturesque and everyone hung out around the bridge. But before you could cross you had to negotiate four feet tall metal spikes across the centre of the road. At the opposite side of the bridge stood the feared customs hut. The customs man was known for stopping poor women who pedalled their bikes from north to south with a few pounds of butter and tea hidden around their middle tied up with twine. These basic commodities were much cheaper in the north and with ten or eleven children to feed this made a big difference. We hated the customs men. But this was the meeting place for all the local boys and girls from both sides of the border. We stood in groups on opposite sides of the bridge and waited for someone to make a move. When someone broke rank and picked out a girl, everyone cheered. Courting couples walked round the twisting paths between the tree-covered slopes leading down to the water and many a grassy dell was occupied by kissing teenagers.

My elder sister Rose and my younger sister Josie were much more clued up about boys than me and were in 'the gang'. There was a shop on the southern side called Kinghams that sold everything and we longed to have sixpence to buy a slider of ice cream. I remember it as the best ice cream of my life, with big wavy trails of raspberry ripple through the middle. I would walk down the village street and at least two windows would be opened, usually by neighbours, shouting, "Margaret, are you going to the river? Will you take our James for a walk?" Or Barry, or whoever they wanted rid of. I had a reputation for being a good child-minder. I grew to really resent it and Sunday afternoon for me came to mean minding children, feeling left out and unfinished homework. This interminable ritual was broken by my sister Rose's discovery of a programme on the wireless called *Pick of the Pops*.

Sunday became the day we made contact with a new world of sound, so different to everything we had heard before. Alan Freeman's suave English voice was one of our first links with the world of pop music. No one had a watch so we would be running into the shop and asking the time, then before five o'clock we would run home and pray Mammy did not have any visitors or that Daddy had not come home from the pub or football.

If this was the case we would beg Mammy to let us take the wireless out to the scullery, a tiny room at the back of the house. Daddy would go mad as the wireless was a precious possession, but Mammy always talked him round. We would sit on the draining board, our ears almost against the radio as we had to keep the volume down. It could just as well have been a voice from outer space.

"Welcome pop-pickers! And now for the Top 30."

We would be agitated with excitement, fighting for the nearest position to the wireless. The reception was always hazy, Freeman's voice racing through the names of the different artists, stopping at the 'Top 10'. We nearly burst with anticipation and threw ourselves around to each tune, constantly being told to keep the noise down.

None of us knew how to dance. This was Ireland and dancing meant jive or Waltz. If we were in the living room we had more space to jump around, but in the scullery we only had a tiny square in front of the larder and we all fought to get it. Jiving was what we really wanted to do, as it was what our big brother and sister were good at. No one wanted to take the man's part because the girls got to spin. My younger sister Marie remembers me telling her she would grow up to be a brilliant Jive dancer as she had long gangly legs and arms and threw herself into it with a passion.

I admit years later to deliberately building her up because I desperately wanted her to dance with me, as Rosie and Josie preferred to dance with each other.

This new music did not lend itself to Jive and we had to improvise, making up steps as we went along. Those I taught myself in that kitchen still serve me to this day: one foot behind the other; one, two, three, four; over and over. We also loved to do 'The Twist' and when my eldest brother Michael brought home a record player we felt we had nearly died and gone to heaven.

"Let's twist again as we did last summer! Come on, let's twist again like we did last year!"

Never was the lino in our house shinier. My whole body shape changed over the first months of discovering that dance. I remember a neighbour saying to Mammy, "Your Margaret has got awful thin." My Mum replying: "It's the dancing. She never stops."

A rare disco gave us another opportunity to dance to pop music and this was liberating as we did not need a partner. But Ireland was dominated by 'Show Bands', England being a million miles away, musically anyway.

When I was sixteen I went to Dublin to train as a nursery nurse where I was locked in at ten o'clock each night. No dancing for me. Other, braver, girls climbed out of their windows and down the fire escape into Dublin, but if they were caught they were instantly dismissed. In the nurses home there was a record player so we had plenty of dance practice. The moves learned in the kitchen were much admired, but I had to dance solo as it was a wild thing that no one could share.

My sisters were still living at home and went every Saturday night to the local dance hall in Castellany. I went every three months when I was allowed home on a long weekend. All the way there on the train I thought of getting ready: what I would wear, who would be at the dance, and who would give us a lift. Those were nights of doing our make-up in the mirror above the fireplace, because it had the best light, and nearly getting roasted. I remember my first 'American Tan' tights, my first mini skirt and the first time I bought my own make-up from the silent domain of the chemist shop.

The dance hall was huge and we would join a clamouring gang of young people queuing to get in. Paying was a big thing, as money was so scarce. A boy traditionally paid for his girl and, as sometimes happened, one of my sister's boyfriends would take pity on me and ask me to come to the dance with them. I never knew if he would pay for me until the last minute. It was a tense moment as he approached the little window to pay; nothing would ever be said beforehand.

"I'll pay for Margaret."

Then I would protest and hope with all my heart he would not heed me. Eventually everyone settled down and we went in, me feeling very relieved. I only had pocket money as I was classed as 'being trained'. What little I had went on absolute necessities.

Our coats were handed into a cloakroom attendant, if we could afford it. Then we were charged with the responsibility of not losing the ticket which was frightening as there were hundreds at the dance.

Our favourite band was 'Big Tom and the Mainliners'; our first cousin was married to the trombone player.

They played mostly country songs such as *Tears on a Bridal Bouquet* or *Gentle Mother*, with every other song being a good Jive number. *Pretty Little Girl from Omagh in the County of Tyrone* was one that got everyone up on the floor. The band consisted of guitars, drums, a trumpet, saxophone, trombone, and Big Tom himself, a great big gentle giant of a man brought up on a farm outside the town.

Everyone in England was swinging to the beat of the sixties but we were Waltzing and Jiving like mad. Boys one side of the hall, girls on the other. The evening started with single girls and couples, but come closing time, the country boys had worked up enough courage to come in. When the hall filled to jam packed-ness, the tension was tangible. Girls were on the look-out for certain boys and vice versa. Basically, everyone knew everyone, or, if you had never seen the lad before, you could go and ask, "Who is he?" of a friend and she would ask someone who would ask someone else and by the end of the night you had his family history. You rarely refused a dance unless the asker was stone drunk. Older girls explained how you had to stay with your partner for three dances and at the end, if he asked you to stay on, you had every right to refuse. Saying no to a grown man was a frightening experience for a 17 year old, and it often led to friends coming onto the floor and rescuing you from the clutches of some drunken 'ejit'.

But if the right boy found you, and your steps fell into place, you joined the flow of dancers with all of the room moving in the same direction and you never wanted it to stop. If that spark of energy fired up between you both and you gave it free rein, soon your heads would be touching, locking foreheads like young stags, embraced in the sweet world of 'Old Spice' and manly sweat. All that was left were some clumsy words shouted above the noise. He might say, "Stay," or just keep holding you and nothing needed to be said. Or he might ask, "Would you like a mineral?" I don't remember seeing alcohol there. You would crush your way to the bar and get red lemonade and a straw. This was often followed with the question, "Will you come outside?" meaning 'to court', which consisted of standing against a wall and kissing. If the boy asked you to go to his car, you always told a friend if you were leaving the hall so if you were gone a long time someone would come looking for you. If the boy asked if you would like a lift home, before you accepted, you made sure he would also take your friends. "Don't forget to ask for a lift and just say can my sister have a lift too, don't tell him that there are four of us." I hated that bit.

I did not know the first thing about getting pregnant; I just knew I loved kissing. Today there are some hair-raising stories shared amongst my sisters about near escapes and we laugh long and hard, but they disguise the reality of a raw and vulnerable time when contraception was unheard of and rape was never mentioned. It was hinted at not to lead a boy on, or get him over-excited - it was always the girl's fault. The whole business was terrifying; only ignorance and hormones made it fun. I knew it was forbidden to touch below the waist, and in my case above, as I was flat chested and deeply ashamed of the fact. So all in all it was a tense and panicky experience.

If you had survived the dancing and recovered your coat, you might well make it to the local chip shop for sixpence worth of chips. If one of you had not picked up a lad with a car, you had to thumb a lift. We would stand on the crossroads and there was never any fear of not getting a lift; eventually a van or an old 'jalopy' would pull up. The driver was usually drunk but we all piled in, and I *mean* piled in, one on top of the other. The singing would start as we careered round bends. The squeal of brakes and the screams of the girls as we stopped at the end of lanes and over bumpy 'boreens' kept the level of excitement at fever point. The last stop was the girl's house who had secured the lift, or the nearest point if they were a good neighbour. If it was the girl she was obliged to stay for a while and 'pay' with some more kissing and touching. Time was usually called by threats of her father watching her come home, or a sister coming out banging on the steamed up windows to warn her of Mammy and Daddy wakening. Maybe a date would be made for next week.

Inside you had to negotiate the door as silently as possible, creaky stairs had to be trodden on lightly and if you made it to the safety of bed - often shared with sisters - the story would be laughed over under blankets or in front of a rekindled fire with tea and toast.

One thing was certain, we all had a great night and slept dreaming of our favourite boy. Sometimes it was tears of disappointment but we all shared the music still alive in our heads and we willed the next dance to come real soon so we could do it all over again.

My Very Special Dad
Sally Wood

My father looks so big and strong in the photo on
the wall.
He was once the strongest man in Britain, of that
I can recall.
He had a very exciting career, of that there is no
doubt,
As a stuntman in the films was what he was all
about.
Early James Bond films are some that I knew,
Scarlet Blade, Khartoum, Ivanhoe to name but a
few.
He trained many horses; taught Omar Sharif to
ride
So this, of course, fills me with oh, so much
pride.
The Black Knight, my favourite film, is top of my
list;
He had an amazing part as they battled in the
mist.
The days when he was home were always
special for me;
He would tell me stories as I sat upon his knee.
He would treat me like a princess and buy me
lots of things,
Take me to the seafront and the park so I could
play upon the swings.
My Dad went to heaven when I was still quite
young,

But I feel he's all around me as his praises I
have sung.
I wonder if he's listening as I read this out aloud;
If he is I'm hoping that he'll feel so very proud.
So if you're passing and you want to see my
Dad,
I'll show you all his photos, 'cos they make me
happy, not sad.

If It Ain't Broke
Janis Thomson

For seven years my husband Doug and I, and
our teenage children Suzy and Jamie, spent
wonderful holidays in Forte dei Marmi on the
Tuscan Coast.

"Let's go somewhere different this year," said
Suzy and I.

"What? Where? And Why?" said Doug and
Jamie. "If you want to go somewhere else you
can find it yourselves!"

Of course, every suggestion was poo-pooed
by them until we came up with the idea of a *gite*
in Britanny, to which they half-heartedly agreed.
The plan was to drive to Portsmouth and then
catch a ferry to St Malo, which was a shortish
distance to our chosen *gite*. However, on the day
before our departure, Doug's car was broken
into and the passenger window smashed. We
were told it could be replaced the next day - it

was - but the wrong model arrived, so delaying us for a further day. Actually this was fortuitous as Suzy belatedly discovered her passport was out of date. In those days these could be temporarily renewed at the local post office. However, as it was a Saturday this required a visit to London.

With high spirits we set out on Monday only to find that the ferry was being diverted to Cherbourg - a four hour drive to the *gite*. Much irritation.

"Told you we should have gone to Forte!"

The *gite* was set in the grounds of a farmhouse and, whilst I fussed over the farmer's many dogs, the others went off to inspect our accommodation. Later I was told that they had to frantically strip the place of stuffed animal heads and other revolting ornaments, knowing what I would have said. In passing, one of the aforementioned dogs, a huge Boxer, developed a massive crush on Jamie. He was duly christened Julian (as in Clary) and called for Jamie every morning.

That first evening we set out in the car to find a local bistro. Such high hopes! The sole restaurant in this dead and alive village only catered for weddings. The one bar always had the same old man sitting outside it. We nicknamed him 'Jeune Jacque' - the liveliest blade in town.

With relief we found a restaurant open in the next village. It looked good enough, we thought. But the staff did not greet us warmly and we were marched through several rooms arriving at a table which had us all facing a blank wall. By this time we were finding everything rather amusing and were not upset, nor particularly surprised to be served with unappetising food and - horror of horrors - tinned vegetables.

So much for celebrated French cuisine! We'll find somewhere else tomorrow, we thought and returned to the *gite* for a glass or two of wine, to be greeted by the sound of a tractor churning up the field in front of us and activating hundreds of mosquitoes from a nearby stream. A restless night followed with a furious Doug leaping out of bed every five minutes in violent killing mode.

"We told you we should have gone to Forte!" chorused the boys.

The next day showed grey through the skylight in our bedroom but we stoically packed a picnic lunch and aimed to chase the sun. We never did find it... Our lunch was eaten huddled together, sheltered by rocks, swatting off sand flies.

After the fourth day spent in this manner, and never having found a decent restaurant nearby, Doug took the matter in hand and phoned his secretary in London to find out where the sun was in France. "Paris," she said, and booked us into a lovely art deco hotel at the newly built Euro Disney. The children were very excited and I was very relieved to be leaving this ghastly *gite* (or 'French git' as I now called it).

By this time, despite regular showers, Jamie had a distinctly mouldy whiff about him that I eventually traced to his ancient wardrobe. He rather liked it, he said! We did not!

The weather in Paris was beautiful. We had gorgeous rooms and the children luxuriated in their fluffy dressing gowns and Mickey Mouse ears and the lotions and potions emblazoned with characters from Disney. We all entered enthusiastically into the whole razzmatazz. As it was the first year, everything was sparkling and new. I became a nightmare mother and made my embarrassed children be photographed with all the characters, although Tigger rather pointedly ran away from me. We saw poor Mickey Mouse being led away by his minder with sunstroke, and Minnie Mouse leaning against a bar in a quiet restaurant chatting with two chipmunks: all illusions destroyed. Our stay there cost us more than the whole two week holiday plus fares to Brittany, but we all agreed that, in the circumstances, it was worth it.

It was distressing having to return to Brittany and Suzy and I wanted to sleep in the car, but were not allowed. The weather had brightened up by this point and the next couple of days were spent reasonably happily, although we were all quite eager to leave. But disaster struck again on the morning of departure. Doug, whilst shaving, nicked a minor vein or artery in his nose, which caused excessive blood loss. Alcohol will stop it, I thought, and whipped out the brandy.

"Ouch," said Doug, and much more, but it did stem the flow for a while. I patched it up as best I could and we set off for the port. On board the ferry, however, the blood started to flow again and this resulted in a visit to the ship's rather unsavoury looking doctor, who inserted a couple of stitches in his nose and bound it up with an enormous bandage, making small passengers either laugh or back away. Jamie, hormones in full flow, had met a rather pretty girl so firmly extracted himself from our group.

"Have you seen the man with the nose?" the girl said.

"That's my Dad," admitted poor Jamie!

In retrospect we were very happy that circumstances had shortened our holiday and there was no question where we would go the next year.

The moral of this story? If it ain't broke, don't fix it!

How To Jog Your Memory
Hélène Meredith

Everything in its place,
Preferably one you can remember.
None of those unreachable spaces
Full of useless clutter.
Wear your glasses on a string;
It may not be fashionable
But it will stop you searching
Forever under the table.

Do the crossword every day;
It might stretch your mind
And keep you occupied
For the rest of your life.
Make a list of what to do;
Don't lose it behind the sofa.
Learn it few by few
And you will go far,
At least, as far as writing it...
Use mnemonics.
"What on earth is that?" you say.
Birthdays, holidays, wedding day
In your mind will stick.
Memorise long numbers,
Divide into sections.
Choose words or pictures
To catch your imagination.
But then, you might forget them too!
Prepare for the unexpected,
Memory can play tricks.
But look unaffected
Even if you feel sick.
Learn something new:
Like a foreign language.
Visit new places
All to your advantage.
Write down your dreams;
Find out what they mean.
Analyse the sub plot
And see what you forgot.
Finally,
Write a poem and make it rhyme.

It may take you ages to find
The right verse in your mind.
In which case, forget the rhyme.

I Remember
Mary Goldfinch

I remember being on a 'Ribble' bus and entering
the village. I saw a wooden sign swing in the
breeze with 'Hovis' written on it. I remember
getting off the bus in the village square. It was
called Red Lion Square because there was a
pub at one side called The Red Lion with a big
lion painted in red above the main doorway.

I remember seeing the house for the first
time. We only had to walk a short distance to get
to it. I was with my parents and younger brother.
The house seemed enormous but it was not big
at all. The garden at the side of the house had
lots of rocks and trees and shrubs. I went into
the dining room and I saw a lamp shade over the
centre of the table. My brother and I soon found
out that we could pull the lampshade down to
touch the table or let it go up to near the ceiling.
It was suspended on a cord with weights which
allowed you to do this. When Mother found out
that we knew how to move the lamp shade she
told us off. So we never did that again. We had
by this time learnt that if we wanted to have a
quiet life, it was best to do what we were told. Of

course we were experts at enjoying ourselves by playing in the garden. So we had a lot of freedom.

I remember my first day at school. My mother took me on a bus and at the edge of the next village the bus stopped and we got off and crossed the road. We entered a garden and walked up a flight of stone steps. Mother rang the front door bell. A short time later the door was opened and we went into a sitting room. A lady about the age of my mother asked us to sit down. I realised quite quickly that the lady was the headmistress of the school. There was a black cat sitting on the rug in front of the fireplace. I was told that his name was Socks because he had white feet and the lower part of all four legs was also white.

The three of us went up a flight of stairs and walked along a short corridor. The headmistress opened a door and there were about eight children and a teacher. One boy was sewing a piece of cloth and somehow he sewed it to his kilt. I saw a big tray on top of a table. There was some sand in the tray and model trees, houses and bridges were carefully arranged to look like a village. There was also a round mirror which I thought looked like a pond. The room was called 'the play room'.

A Sleeping Beauty Town

Hélène Meredith

I was born in Autun, a small town in Burgundy known as 'The Sleeping Beauty' because it looked like a picture postcard and nothing seemed to change over the years. It still bears the traces of a medieval and Roman past. When I go home and see far away in the distance the cathedral's spire above the town, among a forest of trees, it is as though I am taken back into the mists of childhood.

There were five of us: four girls and a boy. I was the oldest of the girls. My first years are just blurred pictures floating in my mind. We lived in a small village on a hill overlooking the town. The house, which had been in my grandmother's family for generations, was built on top of a stream that ran underneath the floor. The stream went all the way down the hill to the town and we used to sail paper boats, leaves, pieces of wood; anything we could find on it. At night, the river lulled us to sleep. I was about five years old when we left the village to follow my father, an officer in the army, to a training school near Versailles. Three years went by peacefully, between school, the Thursday youth club and daily errands to the bakery. When the war with Algeria was declared in the fifties, my father was sent to the front line. I was eight when he was killed, he was thirty-three. My mother decided to go back to Burgundy to my grandmother's flat in Autun.

At the time I did not realise things would never be the same again. In spite of the shock of losing my father, the move was a big adventure and this little town became our solace. Everything seemed easy at school as I had to repeat my year. The house was alive with noise and laughter. My grandmother's apartment was in a house with three floors next to the parish church. To get to it, we had to go through a dark and narrow passageway tucked between a cobbler and a hardware shop. The corridor opened on to a long paved courtyard. Unusually, the first floor was divided in two by a spiral staircase: kitchen and dining-room on one side, toilet on the landing and bedrooms, workshop and drawing-room on the other.

My grandmother, who was a milliner, received her clients in the drawing-room where hats stood on long wooden poles. Pictures of ladies in crinolines decorated the pink and silver-striped wallpaper. French windows opened onto the market place. On the chimney breast stood a bronze statue of Joan of Arc on a horse. I avoided looking at the figurine in the evening shadows when she became a little frightening. Despite the fact that we were forbidden to go into this room, I often sneaked in to try the hats on and pretend I was a lady. One day, I tore a muslin veil and blamed the cat.

At the other end of the corridor was the *atelier* where the hats were made. My grandmother often told us how she went to Paris in her twenties to train with a famous designer. There, she met my grandfather, a wrought iron artist that I never knew. A 'Singer' sewing machine activated by a pedal took pride of place in a corner. On a shelf sat a wooden head that you could expand at will. Near the window there was a long and narrow table where the apprentice, Madame Jeanne, would steam-iron the felt. When you came into the room, a strong smell of glue gripped your throat. After school this smell mingled with the milky chicory we drank. A door hidden behind the wallpaper opened onto what was for us a real treasure-trove: bolts of fabrics, hat boxes, multi-coloured ribbons, buttons of all sizes, feathers, flowers packed into drawers. It was also the place the cat had chosen to have her kittens.

My grandmother was a plump woman, always in good spirits, who loved eating. She often made us strangely shaped doughnuts covered in icing sugar after school. On Sundays, after Mass, she spent all morning cooking. She loved making *Boeuf bourguignon* or rabbit stew in a rich dark sauce. She kept a few chickens at the bottom of the yard. I can still picture her running after one, then later sitting outside plucking its feathers. Unfortunately, after these wonderful meals, there was a lot of washing-up to do. To my mother's despair, she seemed to use all the pots and pans available in the kitchen.

The apartment was heated by a large stove which had to be stoked up every evening, so my mother would send one of the three oldest children to the cellar to fetch a bucketful of coal, and we would always quarrel as to whose turn it was to perform this task. The cellar, which we shared with our neighbours, was black and vast and, since there was no electricity, we had to proceed by the light of a torch. In the winter it was freezing down there, and the knowledge that our mother threatened us with banishment to its depths when we misbehaved only added to our reluctance!

At the far end of the cellar was a sealed door, which, so we had been told, led to a secret underground passage which ran beneath the town, emerging on its far side. The story was that, during Roman times, the passageway led all the way to the Amphitheatre and that lions had been driven through its depths towards the waiting arena, whose ruins are still visible in the modern town.

If the cellar represented the darkness to us, then the attic was by contrast our heaven. Up there all the old furniture, old clothes, hats and other odds and ends which were no longer used were stored. Daylight streamed in through a skylight and in summer it was very warm. My sisters and I transformed it into our own little apartment where we could hold tea parties for our dolls or play shops. I often sought refuge there, reading in the peace and quiet, safe in the knowledge that I would be undisturbed, shielded from my mother's demands for someone to run an errand to the corner shop.

The school was situated just on the other side of our paved courtyard. Every morning and evening the gate of the courtyard would be closed for security reasons and we were obliged to make a long detour through the town in order to get home. However, at midday the gate was always open, which greatly shortened our route and gave us almost two hours of freedom.

Since I had come from another school, the head teacher insisted that I repeat my last year of primary instruction, which actually gave me a head start over the other pupils, but consequently made me rather lazy. I was often to be found day-dreaming during lessons and I still remember my teacher reprimanding me for drawing in my exercise books. Once, I was even guilty of the misdemeanour of dismantling a pair of compasses instead of listening to the lesson.

When the weather was fine on Sunday afternoons we would often walk up to the village where the family had previously lived. We would visit the cemetery to place flowers on my father's grave, and then take the footpath which followed the stream as far as the waterfall, earnestly watching the progress of the sticks we had thrown into the water.

When the surrounding countryside lay spread out at our feet, three landmarks were clearly visible against the sky. The first was a huge stone cross, erected by the grateful inhabitants of the town after the Second World War, because Autun had escaped being burnt to the ground by the Germans. The second, further on, above the ramparts, was a statue of the Virgin Mary on the roof of the ancient Ursuline convent, and the last landmark was of course the cathedral itself, standing proud above the old quarter of the town.

The French writer, Colette, said in one of her letters, 'We would all be so much poorer without our childhood memories." I can only agree with her sentiment and, to use her words again, I would say, "I come from a country which I have left behind."

Birthday
Maggie Wright

It was County Monaghan, Ireland, February 1953 around 7.30 pm. One of the worst blizzards in living memory blew outside. Into this place and time I was born.

Our house was in amongst Monaghan's rolling hills. There were wide steps up from the road to a gate set in a concrete wall, around a concrete yard, and either side of the steps were my mother's rockeries (a stab at modernity). This was a new house built after the war with poor materials. There were no surveyors or building inspectors to check for damp courses or to make sure the roof was watertight. It nearly became our grave. The walls wept water, the ceilings were like sieves; nothing was dry. Peeling wallpaper with buckets to catch drips, my mother was exhausted in the effort to keep damp at bay.

There were heaps of blankets on the beds to keep us warm. My sister Kathleen spent a year in Crumlin, the children's hospital in Dublin, with pleurisy and my brothers Michael and Peter were taken into hospital with suspected TB.

The old cottage on the opposite side of the road was solid with rock and thatch, but was now far too small and was used as an outhouse. The new house was a long one storey house, the kind children draw: a door in the middle, square windows either side, and big pots of red geraniums in the deep set windows. The yard outside had a wall around it and a well house sunk in the corner, with steps going down to the door. Inside was a deep dark square pool of water. I remember the excitement when, on one special occasion, we kept a block of ice cream cold in a bucket suspended in the well. I don't remember eating it, just the amazing excitement of knowing it was inside that cold dark place. At the back was a large vegetable garden and looking to the front were the poor small patchwork fields typical of that county.

Each evening I watched from the wall as the great ball of the sun set at the end of the meadow and I dreamed of being big enough to run over and grab it. When the day came that my brothers and sisters let me play with them in the meadow it happened, by coincidence, to be sunset and my short legs ran towards the object of my desire, imagining how it would feel to finally possess it. I was bitterly disappointed that it kept moving further and further away. I had no words to express my feelings and that memory has stayed fresh and vivid all my life.

Country people never locked their doors; hospitality was offered to anyone who knocked, in the form of tea and bread and a seat by the fire. Over most doors hung a picture of the Holy Family, there as a reminder of the day Mary and Joseph were turned away from the Inn in Bethlehem

As you entered you passed a partition called a door jamb and went directly into the kitchen. A dusky, grainy light from the two deep-set windows either end gave a magical light that met in the middle, illuminating the otherwise invisible particles that filled the air; I loved to watch them dance. The only other constant was the square of light from the open door on the range and the glow of the red lamp lit in front of the picture of the Sacred Heart.

In the house were my mother, my four siblings, and my Aunt Maggie. She and Bridget and Mary were sisters, cousins of my grandfather; they never married. It's a mystery why because they were all lovely women. I wish I knew their story. They took Mammy in when her own mother died in the great Spanish flu in 1918. Worldwide it killed 50 to 100 million people. My granny was in her thirties, married to my grandfather Peter Megan, the best shoe maker in Monaghan; they also had a small farm. She was mother to five children: Uncle Owen must have been around six, Uncle Pat seven, Aunt Kate four, my mother was three and Uncle

John was a baby. This unrelenting childbearing must have been a contributing factor to her poor health.

It was only in the last years of her life that my mother got to see a photograph of her own mother; some distant relative unearthed it. She was very upset about not having a face to remember and she often told us how this became a problem when she was pregnant with her first child, my sister Bridget, so she sought out and spoke with the district nurse who performed the last duties for her mother. Throughout her pregnancy she dreamed of a woman with very long plaits coming to her to tell her that all would be well. When she spoke with the nurse, now very old, she said she remembered her mother in particular, for she had plaited her hair in two thick braids that reached to her waist.

My mother's brothers stayed with their father and the girls went to different relations. Maggie, Bridget and Mary, the maiden sisters who took my mother in, thought they would never have children so cherished my mother: their little Molly. I don't know a lot about Aunt Kate, but she didn't have three mothers doting on her!

My mother married against the aunts' wishes. My dad had no interest in farming, but dreamed of escape and city life. He loved going to the pictures and dreamed of sharp suits and good shoes. They were madly in love; luckily she was fit and strong and had her babies easily. Aunt Bridget and Aunt Maggie helped her with us

207

children, allowing her to do chores around the farm. Aunt Mary went into the town to work in the big hotel.

I was my mother's fifth pregnancy. Uncle Owen, one of my mother's brothers, was the real farmer and did most of the work. He lived with Grandfather just a couple of miles along the road and, as a token of gratitude for caring for my mother since a child, my Grandad lent him out to work on their land.

Dad had no idea of farming but he had a quick brain and was an exceptionally hard worker, always getting quickly to the top in all his jobs. He had to travel all over Britain to work, sending money home. I think he was driven to drink by boredom and frustration; in another place and time he would have succeeded in any job he chose. His father lived in the gatehouse and walked the railway line checking the sleepers from Droomgoose to Dundalk. In those hard times railway workers were the lucky ones; they never went without. They had heat in the form of coal, there were steady wages, and at the end of each day Grandad went to tend his vegetable garden. Both my mother and father enjoyed comfortable childhoods; this was not the best grounding for the hardship in their adult lives.

That week in February there was a tinker man travelling the roads and the people were saying he was to be watched and no woman should be alone with him. Several people had trouble getting him out of the house. My father was not at home as he had ridden into town for messages. Around one o'clock in the afternoon the snow started to fall and as the day wore on, grew steadily heavier. The only other adult in the house was my Auntie Maggie who would have been in her sixties then. My tired and anxious mother was at the end of her pregnancy.

Sure enough around three o'clock a knock came at the door and a great big dishevelled man walked in. His face was covered in a bushy beard and his hair was red, matted and very long. He grunted a greeting and sat down next to the range. My Aunt Maggie made tea and talked to my mother as if Daddy was out in the yard.

"Will you shout down to Tommy his tea is ready? Is he seeing to the animals? Don't worry Molly he will be in any minute; now isn't this weather atrocious?"

She wanted the tinker to believe there was a man about the house. Mammy knew Daddy would not be able to get back from the town on his bike through the snow and she hoped and prayed someone would give him a lift but cars were hardly seen on the back roads. The clock ticked noisily as time passed and the man fell asleep in the heat of the fire; steam rose from him filling the room with his stale smell. As Mammy paced the kitchen looking for jobs to do she felt the first familiar twinge of labour. She could not announce her weakness in front of this unpredictable stranger. My two brothers and sisters eased the tension by playing marbles on the pitted stone floor. By now she had retreated to her bedroom and Aunt Maggie, growing ever anxious, was aware of what was happening. She took my eight year old brother aside and wrapped him in the warmest clothes she could find and sent him out into the snow to run to a neighbour. The Cumiskey's were about five minutes' along the road and up a long lane.

"Tell them to get May."

That was another Aunt. She had no children and was a very, capable hard-working woman. My Aunt Maggie was worried sick about my young brother going out in the storm but shortly after he had left, in walked my father and Aunt Mary. The hotel she worked in had got her a car home; she was awfully well thought of and was getting on in years. The stranger slept on. My father woke him and explained what was happening; he was none too pleased but offered the stranger shelter in the barn for the night and he went outside. The car was sent for Aunt May and a wet and cold eight year old Michael was warmed and brought home to the fire.

After a short time I arrived. Because of the impassable roads, I was not, as tradition dictated, immediately baptised the next day. Usually babies were brought to church as soon as possible after birth in case they died and went to 'Limbo'; thankfully today the Catholic Church has erased this ludicrous notion. Two days later on the 26th I was brought through the snow to the chapel and my Aunt May, who had helped bring me into the world, was my godmother. During the ceremony she stumbled on my second name and the priest who, by all accounts had no patience, said, "Leave it, she will have enough trouble with 'Margaret'."

I was jealous all my childhood of my sisters owning two first names: Mary Bridget, Rose Veronica, Kathleen Elizabeth, Ann Marie, Josephine Geraldine and me, plain Margaret. Those two interruptions, one of weather and one of naming, heralded my arrival into this world.

For eleven years I celebrated my birthday on the 26th February and my godmother always turned up with lemonade and cake. I was very proud of this fact as she was the best godmother of them all. Then I had to apply for my birth certificate and baptismal certificate to go to secondary school. By a fluke it arrived on the day of my birthday and in between the lemonade and cake a conversation broke out among the adults.

Aunt May had a particularly strident voice. "You have it wrong, she wasn't born on the 26th it was the 24th. Don't you remember the blizzard? Sure we couldn't move for snow. It was a couple of days before we could get over the road to the chapel."

Everyone then agreed in the most casual way that they had it wrong. How could they have forgotten the two days of being snowed in? Then the talk turned to the tramp that was in the house. I had been listening with the fascination of a child when their parents talk about memories concerning them. I tried to take in these facts and found my cake didn't taste nice anymore and I felt like crying. No one seemed to notice I was upset and I didn't know how to express it. I think I said, "Mammy don't you remember the day I was born?"

No one paid me any heed; times were different then and children's sensibilities were not so precious as now.

It shook me up and I brooded about it for ages. At 11 years old I was a very sensitive child and something changed in how I saw myself. I became smaller, less important. I had my birthday on the 24th February from then on.

Many years later I think of my poor mother and all she had to put up with and I feel nothing but compassion for her hectic and hard life. A sensitive weepy child was the last thing she needed amongst the demands of her brood of nine.

To this day I have to remember to put the date of my baptism as my birthday as that is what is on both my certificates and I have endless forms returned to me as I automatically write the 24thFebruary.

I thank all the characters that were present on that blizzard-blown day on the 24th February 1953; for welcoming me to the world with the gift of a story to tell; and maybe that is the reason that I have always loved the snow.

The Unopened Letter

Janis Thomson

This story takes me back quite a few years when I was living in St. Albans and both my children were still at home. It relates to letters which should have remained unopened except by the recipient. My son Jamie was just at an age when he was receiving mail. The official ones were addressed to Mr J M Thomson and, as my initials are the same, I very often opened his letters (by mistake, of course!).

"Mum, this letter says 'strictly private and confidential on the front', and it clearly says Mr. Why did you open it?"

"Well, sorry, I thought it said Mrs."

"Yes," he said, unconvinced.

It was, I thought, a reasonable mistake as we were with the same bank so the envelopes had identical marking.

"Why did you give me the same initials as you?" he said, "I bet it was so that you could open my post. If you'd have been really smart you would have called Suzy Jane-Mary instead of Suzy-Mary. You'd have had a field day then!"

This illegal opening of letters went on for a while and I stuck to my rather feeble story. I felt quite guilty and got into loads of trouble but on the other hand, being his mother, I really wanted to make sure he was conducting his financial affairs properly.

One Saturday morning some time later, Doug and I were having a cup of tea in bed and Suzy brought up the post. All for Doug. Most were circulars or bills, but one was handwritten with 'strictly private and absolutely confidential' written on the top. He put them aside, drank his tea, and then went to the bathroom. I looked at the 'strictly'. It was handwritten and the postmark was Watford. Ummm! I don't know anybody who lives there, I thought.

Back Doug came and at last opened his letters, his expression unchanging. "I'm going to get another cup of tea," he said, and left the letters on his side of the bed. I hesitated; the 'strictly' one was on top of the pile. I couldn't resist. If I did it quickly he would never know! Curiously I pulled the sheet from the envelope:

"We knew you would look, you nosey old cow! We knew you would look you nosey old cow!"

Line after line, after line, and then a drawing of what was supposed to be a cow at the bottom. My family were all outside waiting for my reaction, laughing.

Did I learn my lesson? Well, not really.

I later heard that quite a lot of effort had gone into this. Doug had asked one of Suzy's girlfriends to write the envelope, and she had posted it from her home town.

Sundays
Hélène Meredith

Sundays were always special. I can still hear the cathedral's symphony of bells calling people for Mass. My mother insisted we wore our best clothes. I remember vividly the first tailored suits she bought for my sister and me when we were about 14. Mine was mustard and my sister's burgundy red. I wore stockings and a suspender belt and my first pair of high-heeled shoes made of brown suede (more about the shoes later). My sister, who was the sporty type, refused point-blank to wear stockings as she found them very uncomfortable. She much preferred white socks and flat shoes, which looked a bit odd with a smart suit. Both my mother and my grandmother wore hats but we did not have to, except in the winter.

Saint-Lazare cathedral was impressive; it stood in the middle of a small square, dwarfing everything else around it. Built in the 12th century to accommodate the pilgrims flocking to the tomb of St Lazarus, it had a huge Romanesque sculpted tympanum above the doorway, depicting the 'Last Judgement'. As we went through, I always glanced at it. Which side would I end up on? Heaven or Hell? Or possibly Purgatory, if I did most of what my mother asked of me.

On each side of the nave stood enormous pillars decorated with sculpted friezes representing scenes from the Bible. My favourite was 'The Flight into Egypt'. The Virgin Mary on a donkey, holding her baby close to her as Joseph followed behind, seemed so true to life. Above my head hung a cardinal's hat swaying gently in the draught - a welcome distraction during the long and tedious Mass. In the choir young boys, dressed in red robes with white lacy surplices and little red caps, sang in Latin with angelic voices. The church could be quite cold in the winter and Sunday Mass was a lengthy affair. By the time the homily, the collection and the endless procession for communion were over, more than an hour had passed. On our way out, we were rewarded by the organ playing a grandiose and uplifting tune that resounded throughout the cathedral.

Other Sundays, when we were pressed for time, we went to the church of Notre Dame, right next door to my grandmother's flat. I did not like this church. I thought it was dark and eerie. On each side of the nave, the confessionals lurked in the shadows and looked very forbidding. In one of the many alcoves was a statue I particularly disliked. It was that of an old priest dressed in a black robe with a gaunt face and eyes that seemed to penetrate your soul. My sisters used to tease me about it. It had started on a school trip to the town of Ars where the saint depicted in the statue had once lived. We schoolchildren were told that the Devil had set the priest's bed on fire and in my mind some of the evil had somehow rubbed off on the statue. To me it was akin to the 'bogey man' and for a while I had nightmares about it. I used to keep my slippers under the bedclothes so I could get away in case he came for me in the night.

After Mass we sometimes stopped at the patisserie to buy a dessert for lunch: either a big cake or individual ones, depending on our preference. Because my mother was working all week, my grandmother cooked Sunday lunch: an elaborate affair with three courses. The starter was usually quite simple: a mix of tomato salad, shredded carrots in vinaigrette and celeriac *remoulade* with mustard and herbs or *oeufs mimosas* - hard-boiled eggs with their yolks mixed with home-made mayonnaise.

The main course was invariably some kind of meat in gravy. My grandmother adored gravy and I can still picture her, a piece of bread in her hand, wiping it round her plate with relish. The meat dish was either *boeuf bourguignon*, *coq au vin*, *blanquette de veau* or rabbit with a mushroom sauce. My grandmother excelled in making desserts. Her favourite was *diplomate*, some kind of *Charlotte* made out of biscuits soaked in kirsch or rum, layered with redcurrant jelly then chilled and served with *crème anglaise*. Another dessert she made quite often was *oeufs a la neige*, made with beaten egg-whites poached in hot water then fished out and placed on top of custard. She added some pieces of toffee around the eggs and we used to fight for them.

After lunch, rain or shine, we went out for the traditional Sunday *promenade*, usually uphill to

Couhard, the small village where my grandmother lived when she was a child. This is where my new shoes lost some of their appeal. Walking on the cobbled streets I was clinging to my grandmother's arm, trying not to fall, when to my dismay, one of the heels broke off and I had to hobble for the rest of the afternoon with my mother's "I told you so" ringing in my ears.

My mother always said that half of the village's inhabitants were related to us. On the way, we visited one of our many cousins, Jeanne, who worked with my grandmother as a milliner. We brought her a bag of stale bread for the rabbits she kept in the back garden and in return she gave us half a dozen fresh eggs. In the main square of the village was the café-bar owned by Madame Marguerite, another distant relative.

We stopped at the cemetery to put some fresh flowers on my father's grave and to remove the withered ones. Then continued uphill, following the stream along a wooded gully, which was very pleasant and cool in the summer. At the end of the path, we crossed a small bridge over the stream to look at the waterfall, quite impressive in the winter but reduced to a trickle in the summer. When the weather was hot we delighted in taking our shoes off, paddling in the water looking for fish. Opposite the waterfall was a steep rocky ascent that seemed to touch the sky. I remember one particular Sunday my brother and I decided to climb the rocks and race each other to the top, despite my mother's warnings. On the way up I saw a viper sliding among the grass. I ran down as quickly as I could but to my horror the snake seemed to be following me. I never went up the rocks again.

I seemed to be accident- prone when I was a child, maybe because I was easily distracted. One Sunday, we were just coming back from our walk towards the village café, when I tripped by the side of the road and fell into what I later realised was a cesspit. Of course, everyone except me thought it was hilarious. The stench was indescribable - my mother had to use a whole bottle of *Eau de Cologne* to get rid of the smell.

I remember one day standing on a chair, messing about, when I fell onto the tiled floor and gashed my head. I was rushed to the doctor who gave me a few stitches and dressed my wound with a huge bandage. I thought it looked so unsightly that the following Sunday I refused to go to the September fair with my family for fear that people would laugh at me.

When we did not feel like going up the hill, we used to walk round the old city walls. We began our *promenade* behind the cathedral, passing the Ursulines' tower, at the top of which was a statue of the Virgin. The Roman theatre was only a short distance through the town. Once there, we would jump up and down the steps above the arena, or play hide and seek in the caves where long ago lions used to be kept for gladiators' fighting. We then went down towards one of the Roman portals that marked the entrance to the town. On the outskirts was a field with the remains of an old temple with only two walls left standing and what must have been windows at the top. In the field were grazing horses who gratefully accepted our lumps of sugar. I remember my brother caught his jumper on the barbed-wire fence and the horses came over and licked and nibbled his face until we rescued him.

When we were in town, we sometimes visited the dressmaker's house to be measured for new outfits. So that she could adjust the hem of the dresses, we had to stand on a chair and stay very still for fear of the pins pricking our legs.

Back from our walk we had lemonade and cake instead of the usual piece of bread and chocolate that we ate during the week after school. We then settled down to watch television, which in those days was still black and white. There were films with Laurel and Hardy, Charlie Chaplin or 'Cowboys and Indians', which my brother was very fond of. In our plays he was the cowboy hero and we four girls were the Indians, and of course, he always won.

Before we went to bed, we had to lay out the clothes we would wear for school the next day. After so much fresh air and walking, I was usually tired enough to fall asleep quite quickly and dream about the new shoes that my mum might buy me for Christmas...

Where Did That Come From…?

Dancing Through My Youth and Birthday
Maggie says: I have always enjoyed writing but I have neglected it. Belonging to this class has given me an opportunity to explore different approaches to writing. I felt compelled to begin at the beginning to free myself to discover different genres. It is as if the pen connects with a deeper truth and I have to follow it.

My Very Special Dad
Sally says: I find it easier to write poetry than prose. In fact any subject is easier to write as a poem – I think I must be related to Pam Ayres .

If It's Not Broke
Janis says: The Holiday from Hell turned out to be one that we all remember with a sort of fondness, although Suzy and I never dared to go 'off piste' again! I enjoy writing about things that have happened in my family life and it brings back memories for my children, which is the reason I started to write in the first place.

How to Jog Your Memory
Hélène says: I can be quite forgetful at times. I wrote this poem as I thought it might help me remember things."

I Remember
Mary says: I enjoy writing about the past. My memories are very clear and I enjoy putting them on paper. It's for me really, I don't know if others will be interested.

Sleeping Beauty Town and Sundays
Hélène says: I like remembering my childhood in France. I would like to leave a record of it to my children. I hope it makes interesting reading for people who do not know this part of France.

The Unopened Letter
Janis says: it was inspired by an exercise we had in class. Although it was against me, we all found it very funny and I probably deserved it. My new daughter in law is Mrs J Thomson too. She's lucky not to live with me!

Twist Again

I know nothing in the world that has as much power as a word. Sometimes I write one, and I look at it, until it begins to shine. Emily Dickenson

The Perfect Husband
Pat Burt

Skin Deep
Martine Clark

Janet, the GP Receptionist
Michael Forrer

The Vagina Duologues
Pat Burt

My Name's Stacey and I Live in Southwick
Richard Shakesheff

The Perfect Husband
Pat Burt

We were all right until he retired.

The day after he drew his first pension he said, "Now it's your turn for a rest. I intend to take over the running of the house. I'll do all the shopping, the housework, and in time, the cooking. I'll need a little help from you on that. You can just sit with your feet up and read a book or something. Meet your friends for coffee or whatever women do." He smiled and patted my hand. "I'm in charge."

I am sure he meant well, but I like housework. Get a lot of satisfaction from seeing a house looking clean and tidy. I enjoy shopping, looking out for the bargains. But most of all I love cooking - never happier than when I'm chopping and slicing.

My friends told me how lucky I was having such a wonderful man as a husband. They didn't have to sit next to him at mealtimes. He made this awful noise when eating - just the same as my domineering father used to make. For 40 years I begged him not to make the noise. He never made it when we were out or we had company. He saved it just for me. I have even left the table and gone into the kitchen to finish my meal, but he took no notice. Never apologised, just ignored me.

I thought once he retired we would meet friends for pub lunches, but we hardly ever went out because he wanted to cook. I tried going out as much as I could, but that took money and he kept the purse strings very tight. I felt I was in prison.

His idea of cleaning wasn't mine. He vacuumed every day for what seemed like hours, but he never did the corners or pulled the furniture out. He would stop me if he caught me doing the bits he missed.

I was slowly going mad. The eating noises grew louder.

Then one Sunday morning I found myself standing behind him with one of the sharpened kitchen knives in my hand. I was always good at chopping and slicing. Pretty soon he was dripping blood all over the kitchen floor he'd just cleaned.

Would they understand about the perfect husband? At least I'll be used to prison life - perhaps they'll let me work in the kitchens.

Skin Deep
Martine Clark

Sheila felt excited as she walked into the plush beauty salon. She wanted a makeover, it was time to update her image and give herself a new lease of life after being dumped by the gorgeous Tom.

She was greeted by Melanie, the beautician, who said that with the help of a little Botox and some gentle electronic hair-removal from her chin, she would do her best to take ten years off her somewhat tired-looking face.

Sheila, though inspired by Melanie's encouraging words, couldn't help feeling sensitive at being told she looked older and more faded than she felt, but she was here she thought. Let the job begin. First, a lovely facial, then some very painful plucking of facial hair followed by sharp needles pushed into her lips.

God! She felt as though she'd gone ten rounds in a boxing ring. Who on earth told her beauty treatments were painless? This was agony. Finally, she was handed a mirror.

She looked like she had been hit in the face with a saucepan. Her lips were too big for her face and her skin looked like a plucked chicken. There were tiny holes where a few invisible hairs had once been.

"What have you done to me?" She showed Melanie her lips in agony. "Am I your first client? Have you done this before?"

"Oh yes, many times. But never as badly as this." There was a pause as the two women studied each other. "But, as you have been having an affair with my husband, you really picked the wrong salon to come into, dear Sheila."

"Tom? He said he was divorced."

"He always was a liar."

Yes, thought Sheila. Tom must have lied about everything. He not only said his wife was an 'ex' but also that she was a kind-hearted frump, nothing like the woman smiling down at her right now.

Janet, the GP Receptionist
Michael Forrer

"Ouch!" I turned round instinctively. It felt like a small hypodermic needle had been jabbed between my shoulders. Of course no one was there and I repeated to the impatient patient in front of me that there were *no* appointments left this morning, unless he was a *real* emergency, and that *yes* I would ring him if there was a cancellation.

He wandered back towards the car park and I looked at the sun streaming in through the glass doors, momentarily remembering my last holiday before attending to the next person in the queue on the other side of the reception desk. Why did I do this job?

"OUCH!" This time it felt more like something was being screwed into my spine. All the patients waiting were staring at me.

"What's the matter?" I said, but as I spoke I could hear my voice getting deeper and louder. Really loud.

"What is the matter?" I said again and patients put their hands over their ears. My voice had become an unbearably loud mechanical growl. Magazines flew from the waiting room coffee table. A window must have broken - there must be a gale blowing out there, I thought.

I couldn't stop myself. I just had to move forward and in a second or two had left the health centre and was looking down at the coast. I was so high - the two ships heading for the harbour looked tiny. Was I dreaming?

I had always wanted to be a pilot, since I was eight - not a receptionist. But I could not believe this. I looked to the right and saw my arm had extended to an unbelievable size......with two powerful Rolls Royce engines attached. A radio voice as if from Air Traffic Control echoed in my head. "Where the hell has that 747 above Shoreham airport come from?"

The Vagina Duologues
Pat Burt

At the doctor's one Saturday,
Awaiting the jab to keep flu away.
There was quite a queue, mainly men,
Rather unusual, even then.
When suddenly a woman appeared
And stood herself right in front of me.
Tiny person dressed all in mauve
Of every shade, from top to toe.
Her make-up, it was very strange,

As if her features were rearranged
Her eyebrows were shaped as if in fright
Eye-liner nowhere near eyelashes,
Lipstick red, traced as in a bow.
Around the lips, not on them though.
"I must see the doctor I'm in pain."
"This is only for flu jabs," I explain.
Her voice grew louder, "I'm in pain
I need painkillers or I'll go insane."
I looked around, I needed backup.
But backs were turned and ears had shut up.
"I've got arthritis in the vagina."
"Try Nurofen ", I quietly answer.
"What! Pay for it ? I'm a pensioner!"
Off she stormed with rage a-quiver.
All heads turned as if by one.
"Close friend is she?" one man enquired.
"Never seen her before." I quietly replied.
The looks that I got told me I wasn't believed.
Then I heard a voice loudly mutter,
"I wouldn't mind betting that was her mother".

My Name's Stacey and I Live in Southwick
Richard Shakesheff

When I shop at Tesco I always pick grapes, and
then, as I wander the aisles, I'll eat a few as I go.

Sometimes by the time I get to the till there's nothing left of them. Nothing to pay, hey ho!

I'm just waiting for my bus, smoking a cigarette from a pack I bought from my uncle, he works at the airport. Not a brand I recognise, but they're cheap. The bus turns up; I stub the cigarette out on the floor and board it. I flash last week's bus ticket at the lazy driver, and then walk the short way to the seats at the front, marked *For the elderly or disabled*. Why should they get all the perks?

My phone rings, it's Denise calling again. I say *my* phone, well it's not really. I lost my phone when I went out clubbing last week. I know I'm 16 but I look older and fool the bouncers. I found this phone in the park the following day; it's way better than mine. I call that good Karma! I took it to the dodgy phone shop and got its jail broken, now it's got my number. I did use all the credit on the old number first, stupid not to.

Anyway Denise says she's got some cash in hand work for me. I'm always out to make a few more quid, benefits just don't go far these days. I've got the baby to think of too, can't believe he's two already. That's what you get for falling pregnant at 13, I suppose. I hope he's all right. He was sound asleep when I left.

Denise wants me to take some pills to a bloke in Whitehawk for her. She says she'll pay me £20 and my bus fare - little does she know I don't buy tickets that often! I even get a couple of free pills for the weekend, whuh hay!

On my way to Denise's, just got time to send a text to that bitch Lisa Smith. She's been slagging me off on face book. There, that told her. Send: *I'm going to smash your face in.*

Been to Denise's now. She's like a mum to me. Had a big mug of tea waiting when I got there, and even let me have a few puffs on her spliff. Sorted!

Bus is just coming into Hawk now. Shit, there are a lot of police around. Got to play it cool, they won't suspect little me. Oh look, that copper's got a nice dog, not like the ones you see biting people. It's little, looks so sweet.

"Mister, can I stroke your dog? Why's he sat down like that all of a sudden?"
Oh shit, they're going to search me. I grab hold of a handful of pills and stuff them into my mouth, but the filth are on to me already. I kick one in the bollocks, but it's no good, they got me.

This Is Not…
Julie Gibbons

Dear Davina,

This is not an acceptance to return to Stay Slim classes. To be honest with you I found the whole thing purgatory.

Why would anyone put themselves through all that grief to lose a few pounds? I spent hours fiddling around in the kitchen, weighing this and that, and then cutting the food into teeny tiny portions. Chewing every mouthful a hundred times became quite tedious too. Dress it up, as you will, I was never full. I went to bed earlier and earlier with huge glasses of water to try and satisfy my hunger.

Another thing I hated was the weekly weigh-in. I know I wasn't alone in wearing thinner clothes in a bid to appear to have lost more weight. Or making sure I went to the loo beforehand. And I never wore make up just in case.

It was embarrassing, Davina, to hear you say for all to hear, "Clap, everyone, she's done so well this week losing half a pound."

I wasn't the only one to dive into the pub at the end of the road and have a couple of drinks after your classes. John used to say he'd starve the day before just so he could enjoy a whisky.

Anyway, Davina, as I said at the beginning of this letter, the classes aren't for me anymore.

Still, I must tell you some good came from them. I hooked up with John and we've been approached by the model agency Large and Luscious to do some photo shoots.

Funny how things turn out isn't it?

All the best,

Lucy

This is not...
Liz Tyrrell

This is not a letter of complaint
(You know, I'm a tolerant girl)
But how can you fix my computer
From the other side of the world?

I'm a very positive person.
Like you, I'm extremely polite.
But why ask "How are you this morning?"
When it's half past eleven at night!

You tell me of wires and sockets and lights
Slow down please, you're going too fast.
It's "Ma'am" this and "Ma'am" that - my fury
ignites
As instructions go rattling past.

I never was known as a racist
And I'm quite sure you've got a degree.
And I know you've a living to earn like us all
But you're meant to be there TO HELP ME!

And a wee bit of help with your English -
"Backside" is not what we say.
When we're trying to locate the hole for that plug
You could take that a whole different way.

It's the BACK of the modem, now trust me.
(If I hear "backside" just one more time

I'll hop on a plane to stick that said wire
In a place where the sun doesn't shine.)

The Silent Scream
Pat Burt

Linda could not believe her misfortune – a virus
– and, of all the places to get it, in the middle of
the desert in Arizona. She should be on a field
trip from Uni studying the flora and fauna of the
desert. Instead she came down with a vicious
virus that has left her virtually paralysed and
worst of all without a voice. The source was still
unknown, hence she was in a private room and
no visitors. Life could not get much worse.

As she lay there, propped up, with the
machines whirring around her, wondering what
was going on, she was more bored than she had
ever been. Her limbs were not working, but her
brain was still active. The nurse had left the TV
on. Fat lot of good that was, thought Linda. It
was left it on the shopping channel and she
could not use the remote.

Suddenly out of the corner of her eye she
saw a movement – a sort of scuttle – but she
couldn't turn her head to see. Then there was a
'plop'. Looking up she could just make out the
ventilator grill, and coming through it were
spiders. From what she could make out, desert
tarantulas.

Linda hated spiders. In fact she had total
arachnophobia. She was a botanist – the study

of bugs made her shudder, and spiders in particular. She watched in horror as one by one they dropped through the ventilation grill. She heard them scurrying across the floor. She tried to feel for the call bell. It wasn't under her hand. Then remembered the nurse had placed it on the bedside locker when she tided the bed. She'd been called away before she could replace it.

As she looked up, a large fat specimen squeezed itself through the bars. Its red eyes had a glow. This one didn't fall; it clung to the wall, as if to get its bearings.

The scream was there but it would not be heard.

Her eyes flickered, trying to see where they were. Why here? Then she remembered something – they were looking for water. The shower room – would they go for the shower room. One look – the door was closed.

Another larger spider had joined the first.

Slowly they started down the wall.

Linda looked at the water jug on the stand over the bed.

She tried to make her legs move. She tried to scream – but nothing came.

The two larger ones jumped off the wall and crouched as if looking round.

The smaller ones were trying to get under the door of the shower room.

Some were climbing up the door.

The two big ones started to move across the floor towards the bed. They disappeared from Linda's line of vision.

Where was the nurse? She was supposed to be on half hour observations.

Then, at the end of the bed, two feelers appeared, followed by a fat hairy body with red eyes. They slowly hauled their bodies up onto the bed. There they stayed.

Almost thinking what to do next. Smaller feelers appeared. Waving.

Suddenly the door opened. The nurse came into the room, saw what was happening and ran away screaming.

The noise frightened the intruders – and more of them ran onto the bed.

Halloween
Martine Clark

It was Halloween and outside Wendy's kitchen window she could see lots of little witches and ghouls and child skeletons running up and down the garden paths, knocking on doors, getting a sweet if they were lucky.

Wendy loved this time of year. Just one day every year that she could be herself and roam the streets in her favourite black dress and black hat and, if she was very careful, she could jump on her broomstick and fly around. On the odd occasion she would be spotted, but she was very quick and the few people that got a glimpse of her thought it was some amazing expensive device that maybe some little rich kid had been given. But no, it was her beloved garden broom and she was the only one who had the power to make it fly.

How she wished she could do this more often, but she couldn't take the risk. In the old days she would have been burnt at the stake, nowadays she would be labelled a crank or weirdo, someone to be avoided. She had lots of friends and colleagues, and of course, they had no idea of her other identity.

This particular Halloween she was invited to a party by a work colleague. She got ready and admired herself in the mirror. She would be the most convincing witch they had ever seen and not even have to try. The party was in full swing when Wendy arrived. Witches and ghosts and black cats everywhere. She thought it would be fun to fly there on her broom, she didn't have far to go. She arrived and left her broom outside in the garden. It was a very ordinary broom, no one would notice it.

Oh wow, this is fun! she thought as she was handed a drink. It was a goblet and looked like blood, but the taste was bland. Wendy grimaced and suddenly it started bubbling and making odd noises. The other pretend witches were amazed.

"Wow! What's in that drink? A magic potion?"

Exactly, thought Wendy, a very potent one.

"Would anyone like to try some of my hubble-bubble concoction?"

"Ok," said Johnny. He was her boss and had an irritating crush on her.

No sooner had he taken a sip, he was on the floor croaking and looking remarkably like a little frog. This was getting scary, but Wendy was enjoying herself.

"How did you do that?" asked Jenny. They shared the same office.

"Easy, I'm a real witch. I can do anything I like".

She randomly waved her wand around and started turning people she wasn't keen on, into frogs and toads. This was the most fun she had had in years.

The thing was, she hadn't actually done any magic tricks for so long, she couldn't remember how to reverse the spells. There were frogs and toads everywhere.

"Oh, my goodness, I've really gone too far with this".

Wendy waved her wand, muttered strange words but the frogs and toads were everywhere.

Panic set in. There wasn't a human in the room. With her head in her hands and deep in thought, she heard a voice. It was Ben from Accounts.

"Muscas, Nostas, Butas, Bostas," he whispered to her.

"How do you know those words?"

"You aren't the only witch in town, you know. Just say those words and they will break the spell. On the other hand, we could leave them all like that for a while. I've put my broomstick next to yours outside. Let's go for a fly about before we turn them back again."

"Ben, I had no idea."

"Really? Well I've always known about you, Wendy."

They jumped on their broomsticks and flew across town, over the rooftops. This was such fun. This was what being a witch was all about. They landed back in the garden and laughed and laughed.

The next day at work the party was the only topic of conversation.

Everyone said how strange it was that they had all dreamed they were frogs or toads. Wendy and Ben nodded in agreement.

Box Clever

Julie Gibbons

The phone in the box on the corner of the street suddenly began to ring. Reg glanced around, but, seeing no-one, picked up the receiver.

"Well, about time too."

"I beg your pardon, who is this?"

"It's me, of course. Come on, don't play the innocent with me."

Reg was intrigued. "But how did you know I'd be here now?" He heard a snort on the other end of the phone.

"Well mate, you're always on time. You walk the same way to work, you leave the same time.

And I bet you even have the same sandwiches for lunch every day."

Reg went quiet as he contemplated the last statement. It was true. Ham, followed by an apple. "So what I'm about to say may come as a bit of a shock," the voice continued. "I want you to ask yourself if you want to spend the next 20 years going to that office, eating that lunch and going home to the wife, and getting grief from the kids?"

Reg, startled by the question, could only stammer, "But how do you know me?"

"I'm the secret part of you that only you know about, the part that wants to break free."

"Sorry to disappoint, but I'm perfectly happy with my life." Reg knew he sounded pompous.

"Really? Don't you think your wife has let herself go a bit? And your kids, well, I bet they still tap you for money at every opportunity."

Reg thought about it. Mmm, Gloria wasn't as fussed about her appearance as she was when they'd first got together. As for their children, well, adults now, they were always answering back, thinking they knew it all. He sometimes wondered when it had all gone wrong.

"You're imagining that fishing trip to Scotland, aren't you?" The voice butted into his thoughts.

Reg started. "You've read my mind. A week of peace and quiet, a cosy little lodge near the pub."

"Just yourself to think about, eh?"

"Tempting. It would be nice."

Reg felt his shoulders relax just contemplating the idea.

Blow them all. He'd go. He'd march into the office; tell them he'd take some of that holiday he was due. A week or even two. He'd say he couldn't be contacted at all. Let others take some of the flak for a change.

"Are you still there, mate?" The voice sounded anxious.

"Yes, yes, I was just thinking about what you said. I'm sick of always putting everyone before me. I've made up my mind, I'm going away." The person on the end of the phone exhaled softly. "Good on you, mate, you deserve a break. I've enjoyed our chat."

Reg was about to reply, but the line had gone dead.

oOo

Gloria nestled next to Phil in the bed. "God, you should have been an actor. What was all that mumbo-jumbo about the secret part of him? I had to stop myself from laughing out loud."

Phil put his arm round her. "Well, you always said he was into those weird and wonderful ideas."

Gloria tugged at the lobe of his ear. "And what was that about letting myself go? You're a cheeky boy, you are. The only letting go I'm doing is in this bed. Thanks to you we're going to get a couple of weeks to ourselves. He fell for it hook, line and sinker."

Twisting
Martine Clark

Let's twist again like we did last summer, or was
it winter?
Who cares, let's twist again in the sun or rain.
Let's move or shake and let our hair down
Just one more time for old time's sake.
Let's have some fun and get the body moving.
Let's grab someone and really start the grooving.
The bones may creak, the body feels weak
But it's better to twist than dance cheek to cheek.
I'm young again - don't wanna feel old
Just having fun. Let the night unfold.
The jive's quite fast, but I'm doing all right
I hope I last well into the night.
The music gets slow, am I in with a chance?
He looks quite nice, shall I ask him to dance?
He beats me to it. We're dancing slow
Don't know about him, but I'm ready to go.
The nights still young and so is he
I'm ready for some fun.
Naughty old me.

Where did that come from...?

The Perfect Husband
Pat says: the idea came from friend who's newly retired husband had gone to Cookery School and now wouldn't let her near the kitchen!

Skin Deep
Martine says: I adapted this from a real life story but subtly changed it.....

My Name Is Stacey and I live in Southwick
Richard says: the story came out of a class exercise when Bridget asked us to write about someone who commits a crime every day. Stacey commits lots of crimes!

Janet the GP Receptionist
Bridget says: this story grew out of a class I gave on magic realism. Michael selected a character from a sheet of photographs I handed out and made the following notes *Janet. Born in Woburn, Bedfordshire. Receptionist. Cheerful. Loud. Sociable. Smart appearance - recently permed hair. Mid 50s. Not sure where she is going in life. Works at Portslade Health Centre. Lives in Woodland Drive – "the speed humps are such a nuisance." Likes the woods and path at the end of her garden.*
Legend has it that film director Mike Leigh asks all his actors – including those with non-speaking parts – to understand their characters to such an

extent that they know what they did on their 8th birthday. Michael decided that on her 8th birthday Janet had a party with 12 friends and went to the park. She wanted to be a pilot.

I also asked each writer to describe what was in their character's purse or wallet. Michael said that Janet had some Euros left over from her last holiday that she kept in hope of the next. Once the character was firmly established the story could begin… with an itching sensation around the shoulder blades.

Vagina Dualogue
Pat says: this happened to me whilst waiting for my flu jab. I was the only woman in the queue. I am sure that they didn't believe me when I said I've never seen her before.

This is Not
Bridget says: Julie and Liz wrote their own version of Paul Hansford's poem *This Is Not A Poem*.

The Silent Scream
Pat says: this would be my worst nightmare - not sure where the idea came from, but I wish it would go away!

Halloween
Martine says: this came about after a class discussion about things that are spooky and it

got me thinking…

Box Clever
Julie says: I can't remember where the idea came from!

Twisting
Martine says: I wrote this after we decided on our book title.

Trip the Light Fantastic

You can't use up creativity. The more you use, the more you have. Maya Angelou

Garden Talent
João Sousa

Poetic Licence
Liz Tyrrell

The Straw That Broke The Camel's Back
Christine Maskell

What Do I Like About Painting?
Hélène Meredith

Daft Definitions
Julie Gibbons

Sleeping Beauty
Hélène Meredith

Landscapes
João Sousa

The Worst Thing That Could happen in a Creative Writing Class
Charlie Bowker

Garden talent

João Sousa

Words arrive silent
Take their place
Giggle
Rub shoulders with
Imaginary sounds

Near by
Background music
Sprays insinuations,

The ballet of words begins
Emotions, memories, insights.

Like a platoon
The poem stands to attention
And then
Disbands

Poetic License
Liz Tyrrell

I'm trying hard to write some verse
'Iambs' or 'trochees'? What a curse!
It's hard enough to make it scan
You want rhyme too? Well, if I can.
The metres are all Greek to me.
Take 'Pyrrhic', empty victory.
The 'dactyl' is an ancient bird.
Of 'amphibrach' I've never heard.
I've eaten 'anapaest' in Rome
and climbed the 'Trochees' far from home.
My mind resembles an abyss
I won't earn 'spondees' doing this.

The Straw That Broke the Camel's Back
Christine Maskell

For weeks the campaign had raged. He had burned the midnight oil getting all the statistics together and now he was ready. The speeches had been made, the leaflets distributed and there was nothing to do now but wait. He was like a cat on a hot tin roof, as he straightened his tie nervously. Armed to the teeth he had left no stone unturned, tonight was the calm before the storm. He felt dog tired, but it had been worth it.

He'd not be the one with egg on his face after tonight, he thought! Beyond a shadow of a doubt, he now had a wealth of information on the competition; enough to send them up a creek without a paddle.

It had been a whirlwind campaign, no doubt about that and until Jenny had come on the scene, he'd been like a bull in a china shop. She was a walking encyclopaedia and could really dish the dirt. The campaign had come on in leaps and bounds since she had arrived and, although his speech would bring on a storm of protest, it was just the tip of the iceberg. She had been a tower of strength and he knew he was head over heels in love with her, but their personal life would have to wait until after the election. He wasn't one to lead someone up the garden path, not at all, and Jenny had a heart of gold, she'd understand. He didn't want to count his chickens before they were hatched, but this time it was in the bag – on the council and engaged to be married!

He had totally forgotten the eviction from one of his numerous flats in a particularly run down part of Brighton. The couple were from some godforsaken country at war, but who actually cares! Charity begins at home so, no rent, out you go! This had been his effective dogma for many years; he'd grown quite rich on it actually. He smiled at his reflection in the mirror. I feel like the cat that's got the cream; and he walked out towards a large room where people were gathering.

Afterwards, he couldn't remember the exact moment the realisation had hit him like a ton of bricks. All he knew was that his carefully engineered campaign, which had cost him an arm and a leg incidentally, had fallen on deaf ears. People seemed more concerned that a couple of nobodies were joining the flotsam and jetsam that littered Brighton's streets. What a storm in a teacup! People who had been as keen as mustard when he was flashing the money around, now looked the other way. Even Jenny had slapped his face in public and ran off crying and saying she never wanted to see him again.

Well, he thought, as he nursed his fourth whisky, one swallow doesn't make a summer, and tonight's failure is just a drop in the ocean of life. I'm a glutton for punishment so I'll try again next year.

What Do I Like About Painting?
Hélène Meredith

Looking at trees through my window
I can stop the seasons changing.
Objects come alive.
Still life, photographs, flowers
Blossom beneath my fingers.
As the hand that paints starts to shake,

Even a spill over the page
Seems to thrive.
I like the challenge of water,
The reflections of trees in the river,
The constant quiver of waves and ripples,
Highlights on the crest of the sea.

Most of all, I like sunsets.
Pink meddling with the blue horizon,
Yellow hiding behind the clouds,
Burnt orange with purple undertones.
Then darkness falling like a shroud.

Daft Definitions
Julie Gibbons

ANTACID: bad tempered female relative
BULLRUSH: stampede of bovine creatures
CRISIS: sibling cruelty
DILUTE: woman proficient on musical
instrument. See also SALUTE and POLLUTE
EXAMPLE: body after gastric band fitting
FUNGI: lads about town
GARIBALDI: slang for men who lack hair
HURRICANE: desperation of person with
walking stick to move faster
INVOICE: person able to sing in harmony

JUNKET: an object so horrid it must be discarded
KINGCRAFT: ship specifically used for a monarch
LOOFAH: distance from public lavatories
MORTAL: a desire to be a good height
NOSEGAY: an attractively shaped nose
OBLAST: minor swear word
PARSNIP: a male, head of house, barber
QUADRANT: argument in grounds of public school
RINGER: person fond of Church bells
SOFFIT: compliment paid by young people
TRIABLE: competent at riding three wheeled cycle
UNIPOD: only one pea in this pod
VANISHING CREAM: witches' potion
WHIRLIGIG: band that plays fast music
X-RAY: runner-up of popular TV programme
YELLOW: whisper
ZORILLA: cross between zebra and gorilla

Sleeping Beauty (inspired by the painting *Flaming June* by Frederic Leighton)
Hélène Meredith

Asleep in the warm afternoon
You dream about the moon.
Oblivious to the painter.

Shy princess in a tower
Ribbon hair like a cardinal sin
Over a seemingly flawless skin.
The sun burns your golden dress
Like a ball of fire at rest.
Did you pick the deadly flower?
Oleander leaf on the mantelpiece,
Fragile link between death and sleep.
Smouldering in the summer heat
Your body, like a swirling sea
May rise again before eternity.

Landscapes
João Sousa

A road of insecurity
Leading into dark woodland
Blown by wind.
The sound of steps on gravel
Grass crushed under soles of worn shoes
Clouds soak into the mind.
She weeps.
Do you smell the breeze? And
Touch the moisture visiting the skin?
Tree branches wave furiously
Hypnotise your eyes,
Instilling fear.
Do not lose balance! Firm
Your feet on moving sands;
The desert will sweep away your tears.

Silence cracked by thunder.
Echo waves die on silent notes.
The season stamps its dues.
Liquid, the water pours, drilling into the soil
Gentle waves lick the shores of the lake
Lost ducks float aimless.
The fish migrated seasons away.
The rain imports butterflies
And locusts.
The children baking cakes out of dust
Will watch their bellies grow.
Men wander aimless
Busy leaving traces
On the wind
Their footprints erased by sweat.
The rain of tears make
Flowers grow on fat cactus.
Torn sandals expose the sores
On women's heels
Their babies hang from floppy breasts
The hips marking rhythms of faded hope.
The concrete grew into the
Winter days
Dressed with metal windows.
Men foster these lifeless mushrooms.
Do monitor the gymnastics of the revolving
doors.
How come the walls do not
Expand and shrink
As living lungs?
Colourless,
Humanoid figures move in,
Faceless

They pour out.
The air grows stale.
She looks away. The window
Escapes the reach of her jewelled limbs
There is sadness traced on the lines of her eyes.
The child plays white cold
Under the lunch table.
Symphony
In blue
Yellow
Grey
Sunlight pierces clouds
The sky above
Eyes the earth with sad shadows
Holding the brush
The canvas whiteness waits.
The colours melt.

The Worst Thing That Could Happen In A Creative Writing Class
Charlie Bowker

Nothing happened. Nothing.

The Great Creator in the Sky had finally got tired of all the footling about with the new gadgetry: endless virtual realities, headache-making flashy ads popping up on the internet, international twitterology that stopped him from sleeping and the real birds from hearing themselves sing, and all the other general modern abuse that spoiled the innate, pure forms of human creativity that he had taken so many centuries to nurture. So he turned the key on the big machine in the sky that connects to all the children and people's creativity, until it was in the off position.

Bridget came to the class and could say nothing.

Amidst the hundreds of idea juggling in her brain, she particularly wanted to explore the new Edna O'Brien memoir, but, as she put her books down on the desk, it was as though a powerful drain had sucked out all her imagination. Holding the table with both hands to steady herself, all she could say was, "The bus was late…Write a Story…."

She sat down with the shock realisation that her brain had reluctantly dispensed the only two thoughts she had. She was now thinking precisely nothing.

Julie came up the stairs to the classroom, full of the joys of life and looking forward to lunch with a friend in Marks and Spencer's in Churchill Square. But, when she sat down, she could think of nothing to write. Her brain and joy had been sucked dry.

Sallie had been pondering on the experience of the Polish people displaced by Nazi Germany, reliving the traumas of the past in an alien country with no context of their roots. But when she came to open her notebooks, there was nothing there. All she could think of, the last drop of thinking left in her head, was, "It's hot today."

João looked mournful as, wiping his glasses, he searched in vain for the intelligence that seemed to have flown off into the African veldt that he had been remembering. Meanwhile, Pat - who had arrived with a bundle of funny stories and sharp observations about the ironies of human behaviour - started with her usual good humoured smile and decided she would soon get the class's shoulders heaving with laughter. She opened her mouth…nothing…absolutely nothing. Her mouth stayed open with the shock of having nothing to replace the full-bodied humour that she had in her possession only ten seconds earlier.

The creative writers looked at each other in horror; their emptiness was reflected in each other's emptiness and therefore provided no stimulus or interest. Bridget felt somewhere deep inside her a sense of responsibility stirring, as the class leader she ought to get things going. But then it stopped stirring, and she began to wonder, like the others, why she was there and what she was doing.

The coffee bubbling away in its pot for the half time refreshments was more interesting and stimulating than they were….

They went home early…Silently. Lost. With nothing to say…

Bridget shut and locked the door, as she went downstairs to cancel the afternoon class she realised that nothing would happen there again. Not tomorrow, or next week, month or year…

Where Did That Come from…

Bridget says: The title of this section comes from a line in Milton's poem *L'Allergro* that describes dancing.
'Come, and trip it as ye go,
On the light fantastick toe.'

There was also a popular song in the late 1890s that included the lines:
'Boys and girls together, me and Mamie O'Rourke
Tripped the light fantastic
On the side-walks of New York'.

The Straw that Broke the Camel's Back

Bridget says: I asked the class to cram as many clichés into a story as possible – normally not something I would touch with a barge pole – but I thought it would illustrate that clichés are metaphors that have died from over work and should be allowed to rest in peace. Christine came up trumps with this story….

What Do I Like About Painting?

Hélène says: I loved drawing when I was at school. Due to illness, I had to retire from nursing earlier than I thought I would and I took up watercolour painting to fill some of my days. I find it very therapeutic and there is something magical about it.

Poetic licence

Liz T says: Apart from doggerel and poems in friends' birthday cards, I'm not a writer of poetry (though I enjoy reading it). When we were introduced to the correct phraseology it was 'all Greek to me!'

Daft Definitions

Bridget says: Julie came up with these definitions after I gave the class extracts from *The Devil's Dictionary*. Published at the beginning of the 20th century by the American writer and journalist Ambrose Bierce, it hasn't been out of print since. It includes many literary gems such as: Lottery: A tax on people who are bad at math.

Landscapes

João says: I was inspired by visits to the National Gallery rooms of XIX and XX century masters. The poem points to discovery, questions and the search for meaning and purpose. It invites the reader to bring his/her emotions and contributions to the text.

The Worst Thing That Could happen in a Creative Writing Class

Bridget says: I set this as a class exercise but wasn't expecting Charlie's tongue-in-cheek vision of creativity stopping abruptly one Thursday morning just as I am about to mark the register. It's a reminder just how important imagination is in our daily lives.

Authors

CHARLIE BOWKER
Charlie has an English Literature degree from Oxford University. He worked and published and lectured about progressive inner London Social and Community Work and Social Justice. He is currently writing a four volume work *The Land of the Free Across the Pond,* spanning from 1971 to the future.

PAT BURT
Once a member of the WRNS, Pat has worked at ATV film department and been a 'Trolley Dolly' for BA. She has also run a Student Travel Offices. After qualifying as a graphologist in 1985, she has taught and been a conference speaker on the art of analysing handwriting. Now semi-retired, she looks at writing in a different way - creatively.

LIZ CARBONI
Liz moved to Brighton ten years ago after a long and varied career in property development and Estate management in Central London. Her travels have taken her to many places, but North Africa has provided her with tales and adventures that form the basis of her 'almost completed' first novel.

MARTINE CLARK
Born in London, Martine trained as a hair stylist in Knightsbridge before moving to Spain where she managed a salon. After settling in Brighton, she started creative writing classes eight years ago and has recently married her partner of 21 years. They now live in Upper Beeding close to her adorable daughter and granddaughters.....

MICHAEL FORRER
Having retired from the obligations of writing business reports, Michael decided to unlock the door to his imagination again and joined the creative writing group. Many, but not all, of his stories have a health related theme.

JULIE GIBBONS
Julie worked in the Special Needs department of Westdene School in Brighton for 16 years. She enjoyed writing compositions as a child and attended a couple of creative writing classes before joining Bridget Whelan's class. She has had one 'True Confession' accepted for publication and is keen to have further short stories published.

MARY GOLDFINCH
Mary is the widow of a professional engineer. She has a son and three daughters and twelve grandchildren and a step grandson. She was a physiotherapist until she got married. She then

became a secondary school teacher teaching maths in south London.

ROSALIND JOHNSTON
Rosalind translated Holocaust survivor and poet, Paul Celan's work while studying for a Masters in German in the late 1970s, with poems appearing in Poetica in 1989. Recently, her own poetry has been published in SOUTH, and features in the Southbank Poetry Library. At present, Rosalind is completing her first novel.

CHRISTINE MASKELL
Since retiring from the voluntary sector, Christine has begun ticking things off her 'bucket' list'. That includes teaching English for a couple of years in Russia, learning German and currently seeking to extract the book that is in us all.

HÉLÈNE MEREDITH
Born in France, Hélène came to England in 1970s. She fell in love and married an Englishman, working as a nurse for the NHS and her local hospice until she retired. Favourite past times include travelling, watercolour painting, reading, writing poetry and stories based on her childhood.

SALLIE A SAWICKA
Sallie has lived in Brighton and Hove most of her life. She was an auxiliary nurse at the local Children's Hospital before training as a primary school teacher. She taught all subjects –

including football! She married a Polish Army veteran and has two grown up children and four grandchildren.

RICHARD SHAKESHEFF
Richard grew up in Poole, Dorset. A passion for property drew him into estate agency before landing his dream job as a travelling salesman in America. He later joined the Police, initially in Dorset, and later in Sussex, serving a total of 20 years in various roles including Tactical Firearms.

JOÃO SOUSA
João plays with words, language structure, and imagination, moving between his native Portuguese and adopted English. From his meditation practice he built a wider receptivity to every detail of the universe and a connection to every living or inert being. Reality has the substance that the observer places on it - yet no substance is to be found. However, the observer - the scriber - displays a jigsaw of material and immaterial elements and the sounds of those words may cause a wave in response. When this works, he touches the reader; when not, he insists that it is the reader's fault.

JANIS THOMSON
Jan has always enjoyed reading but never wrote before joining Bridget's creative writing class two years ago. Initially her purpose was to write a memoir for her children and, although this is still

the case, she finds her interests have been diversified by the exercises set in class.

LIZ TYRRELL
Liz has taught for as long as she can remember and, after 30 years as an infant teacher, she currently teaches English as a foreign language. She has been writing since she could hold a pencil. Liz won first prize in the 2014 national short story competition organised by West Sussex Writers.

SALLY WOOD
Sally was born in Brighton and lived in Australia. She worked for many years and has a family. Whilst attending a creative writing class with Bridget as part of a Heritage-funded oral history project she contributed to *Knock On Any Door*, a history of the Tarner area of Brighton. She is a director in the family business and volunteers at the Martlets.

MAGGIE WRIGHT
Maggie trained as a nursery nurse in Dublin and then worked as a nanny in London. Her particular love is special needs children. Married with four children and six grandchildren, she graduated from Sussex university aged 49, in English literature CCS.

BRIDGET WHELAN editor.
Bridget is a novelist, prize winning short story writer and creative writing lecturer who has

taught on undergraduate courses and in adult education. Her bestselling book *Back to Creative Writing School* contains 30 writing exercises and is available on Amazon.

http://bridgetwhelan.com

Martlets Hospice

A martlet is a mythical bird that is in perpetual flight which is why they are usually shown without feet. They represent hard work and perseverance and reflect the hospice's ethos of never resting and always responding. The hospice was born out of the merger of three separate charities in 1997, hence the three martlets in the logo.

The Martlets cares for people affected by terminal illness, living in and around Brighton and Hove. It has an 18-bed In Patient Unit, a Hospice at Home service, Patient and Family Support team and provides Therapeutic Day Services for patients and carers living in the local community. It helps patients to live life as fully as they can, right up until the end. Over 24,000 local people have been cared for since 1997.

The service is free, but the hospice is not part of the NHS. In the financial year 2013-14 it must generate over £4.3 million to continue. Less than a third of this funding comes from the NHS so every donation is important. Without community support they cannot survive.

Acknowledgements

Norma Curtis
An award-winning novelist, writing mentor and former chair of the Romantic Novelists Association, Norma volunteered to turn the manuscript of *Dancing with Words* into an ebook and a print book. Without her generous help, this project could not have happened and we want to put on record how grateful we are for the many hours of hard work she has donated. Norma has written a film, short stories and articles on writing-related subjects and has earned an impressive reputation for the expert advice she gives to emerging writers which manages to be both straight-talking and confidence-building.
http://www.normacurtis.com

There are many other people and organisations we wish to thank. Some are listed here. You will find more on our website
http://strictlycomewriting.wordpress.com/

Thank you all for your practical help, support and encouragement.

Attila the Stockbroker
A sharp-tongued, social surrealist rebel poet and songwriter, Attila started as a punk bass player and took to the stage as a performance poet in

1980. Before long he was on the front cover of Melody Maker and is rightly proud of the fact he has earned his living as a poet since 1982. He has performed in 24 countries across the world and is a co-founder of Glastonwick Festival, celebrated in West Sussex every year. He has released more than 20 music/poetry albums and written six books of poetry.
http://www.attilathestockbroker.com

Colleen Slater
The photograph on the front cover is by Colleen, a professional freelance nature and portrait photographer who has generously allowed us to use the atmospheric picture of Brighton bandstand for free. Colleen is an Associate of the Royal Photographic Society and her work is regularly shown in international exhibitions. You can find more examples of her creative work at
http://www.colleenslaterphotography.co.uk

Crown and Anchor
On the A23 - one of the main roads into Brighton - the Crown and Anchor opposite Preston Manor is one of the most tastefully decorated pubs in Brighton, famous for its friendly staff and the welcome it gives all sections of the community from children to pool players to those who have to stick to a gluten-free diet. It has disabled access and free parking as well as excellent food. The Crown and Anchor, 213 Preston Rd, BN1 6SA 01273 559494

Dom Shaw

Dom began his media career at 21 by winning the Grierson Award for Best Documentary. After a few years directing music documentaries for the fledgling Channel 4, he started scriptwriting for television, writing for peak time series on the BBC and ITV networks in the UK. His first novel about George Orwell *Eric is Awake* was published in 2013.

Edward Milner

Edward is a professional ecologist, with many years of experience writing and making films. At the BBC he produced films for the acclaimed Natural History Unit and is now an independent producer. He is also an author, writing *Trees of Britain and Ireland* (Natural History Museum, 2011), contributing articles to the national press and specialist magazines and writing fiction.

PACA Portslade Adult Learning

An adult education college passionately committed to improving the lives of local people, it provide courses for learners aged 19 and over at three centres; the PACA 6th Form College, Boundary Road Learning Centre and Foredown Tower. The courses offered include vocational subjects and those studied for interest and personal development. They range from Pilates and cake decorating to bookkeeping and Mandarin Chinese.

For more information contact Portslade Adult learning at Chalky Road, Portslade, Brighton, East Sussex BN41 2WS
Email:comed@paca.uk.com
Website: www.portslade.org

Portslade Village Centre

Overlooking the idyllic village green, the Centre is a hub of activity for the local community with a particular emphasis on youth work. The Centre's friendly and supportive staff make everyone feel welcome and we would like to thank them for being a home to our weekly creative writing class.
Portslade Village Centre, Windlesham Close, Portslade, Brighton, BN41 2LL

Rob Marks of Ghost Walks Brighton

Actor and master storyteller, Rob will take you on the famous ghost walk around the oldest part of the city to tell you macabre tales of murderers and wandering nuns, hideous apparitions and boisterous poltergeists. The spine-chilling walk takes place throughout the year on Tuesdays, Wednesday, Thursday, Friday and Saturday evenings.
To find out more visit
http://ghostwalkbrighton.co.uk

Suzanna King

Suzanna works for Friends Families and Travellers, a charity working to end racism and discrimination against Gypsies and Travellers and to protect the right to pursue a nomadic way of life. In response to the widespread problems of bullying and discrimination faced by young Travellers, Suzanna wrote and directed a play for children *Crystal's Vardo* about a girl's journey through Romany history and her quest to piece together the shards of her own history. The play premiered at The Pavilion Theatre in Brighton as part of Gypsy Roma Traveller History month and runs popular school performances. To find out more visit **http://www.gypsy-the traveller.org/resources/gtrhm-2014/**

Printed in Great Britain
by Amazon.co.uk, Ltd.,
Marston Gate.